Run to the Mountain

G·K Hall &C⁰

*Also by T. V. Olsen
in Large Print:*

The Burning Sky
Canyon of the Gun
Deadly Pursuit
Eye of the Wolf
The Golden Chance
Haven of the Hunted
Keno
Lone Hand
The Lost Colony
McGivern
Savage Sierra
The Stalking Moon
Starbuck's Brand
Treasures of the Sun
Under the Gun

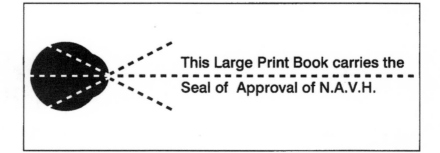

T. V. Olsen

Run to the Mountain

G.K. Hall & Co. • Waterville, Maine

Published in 2002 by arrangement with Golden West Literary Agency.

G.K. Hall Large Print Western Series.

The text of this Large Print edition is unabridged.
Other aspects of the book may vary from the original edition.

Set in 16 pt. Plantin by Al Chase.

Printed in the United States on permanent paper.

Library of Congress Cataloging-in-Publication Data

Olsen, Theodore V.
    Run to the mountain / T.V. Olsen.
      p. cm.
    ISBN 0-7838-9780-4 (lg. print : hc : alk. paper)
    1. Large type books.   I. Title.
PS3565.L8 R8 2002
  813′.54—dc21   2001051963

Run to the

Mountain

CHAPTER ONE

All morning long, blackening clouds had built like cobbled towers above the saw-edged peaks to the north. By noon they came driving down on the foothills and broke in a bleak wet fury across the parched timber and grasslands. The storm caught Bowie Candler on an open meadow, and he raised his face to it and cursed it with a tired tonelessness.

He was already chilled to the bone; he could hardly feel his fingers. Particularly the ones on the hand locked around the horn of his saddle, whose weight made a spreading ache across his shoulders. He had been toting it all morning and he was just about done up. His feet in their cowman's boots hurt like hell.

Jesus H. Christ. Bowie's disgust turned savage; his swearing voice husked into a snarl.

It wasn't enough that that goddam cat had spooked his jughead roan out of camp last night. He hadn't seen the cougar, hadn't had an inkling it was close by, till its high scream had set his horse lunging at its tether. Before he could reach it, the worn rope had parted and the horse was drumming away into the night. Nothing to do then but huddle by his fire and catch snatches of sleep till darkness had grayed to a sallow dawn and made enough light to track by. It was mid-morning when Bowie had come on the horse's

7

remains. The cat he'd heard, or another one, had gotten the animal; wolves had been at the carcass later on. Only raw bones and shreds of flesh and hide remained, along with enough tracks and other signs to tell the story.

So he had started tramping. He wasn't sure exactly where he was, but that didn't concern him too much. He could rough it off the country like an Indian if he had to, though he hated being reduced to such an extremity. There was plenty of game, besides edible roots, herbs, and barks if a man knew what to look for. The only real danger that the high country held for someone who knew it was its howling deep-snow winters, and this was still early September. What graveled hell out of Bowie was the whole stinking run of his luck.

The rains slashed in fierce gusts at his leaning body as he plodded on. He was quickly soaked to the skin, his whole body numb with cold and wet. Thunder pealed, caroming back and forth between the hills. Flickering tongues of lightning played below the clouds. Again Bowie raised his face to them and swore. Of all the Christ-bitten damned luck. He felt the bleak, despairing rage of a man whose load of bad fortune had been topped by a final breaking straw. And there was nothing to curse but the uncaring elements.

It had taken him three days to cross the mountains from K-town, the mining and ranching settlement at the north base of the great Elk range.

Two months ago Bowie had sold his pack horse for tools and a stake to undertake a spell of lone gold-grubbing up on the high range. Five days ago, he'd returned to K-town with a few miserable ounces of color to show for his weeks of labor. After going on a well-earned drunk, he had awakened in an alley with a splitting head to find that his poke had been lifted.

All the local ranches had their full quota of hands for the fall roundup, he'd soon found, and his only choice was to drift out of the country and seek other prospects. Which meant southward, for the fall frosts were already gripping the high country and he wanted to winter warm. Bowie hated cold weather more than anything: legacy of a childhood spent shivering in a share-cropper's shack for what had seemed endless months every year.

Ahead of him, the meadow sloped down toward a storm-whipped stand of aspen. Little shelter there, but at least the trees would break the rising wind. He reached the timber and plunged into it till he found a small glade. Here he crouched in sodden misery, flexing painful sensation back to his numbed right arm and shoulder as he waited for the storm to buck itself out. Wind and wetness hissed through the tree-tops; rain plunked on the drooping, wanly yellowing undergrowth. It dripped, glistening, from the greasy downcurl of his hatbrim; it runneled icily through every tatter in his old canvas mackinaw.

9

Bowie beat his unfeeling hands together till he could move his fingers, then rummaged through his worldly possessions: saddle, bridle, soogan roll, battered Winchester, saddlebags containing any range rider's odds and ends. He'd discarded his worn-out gloves and slicker a week ago, anticipating that he would buy new gear in K-town. At least he'd hung onto the ancient mackinaw, but it was so full of holes, its buttons long gone, that not even the greasy filth which coated it kept the wetness from working through.

His belly was growling with hunger pangs. And his grub was desperately low, as he'd had no money to buy supplies in K-town. Groping in the bottom of a saddlebag, Bowie found a few dirty strips of jerked deer meat. He mouthed one, slowly chewing its rancid hardness to a fibrous pulp that would slide down his throat. What the hell was he going to do now? Just keep dogging it south, he guessed, till he came out of the foothills. There were supposed to be roads and settlements below the southern Elks, and he was bound to hit one. But when? He knew this country only through what he'd been told. Several large outfits claimed most of the high and valley range hereabouts, for the tide of homestead migration had washed around these mountainous pockets. Hustled out by the big augurs or quickly broken by the brutal climate. . . .

Have to hunt up any sort of work he could get, Bowie bleakly decided, any short-term job that would tide him over. Swamp out saloons or stables if he had to. That was another old story with him. He peered at the sky. The storm was slackening to a timid drizzle and he might as well be humping along. Christ, he was tired. But a man might as well catch his death walking as squatting. Briefly he toyed with the notion of abandoning his dilapidated saddle, but figured he could wrestle it through the rest of today anyhow. Or did till he heaved to his feet, lifting the rimfire hull and slinging it across his back. Every ache in his body pulsed back to throbbing life. Pain shot into his calves, and his feet felt like dead blocks as he slogged stubbornly down the slope.

From somewhere below, a horse's thin whicker drifted.

Bowie halted, a faint excitement lifting in him. Horses? Well, by damn.

He trudged on till the trees began to thin away, then halted again. He was on the brink of a long valley of wild hay studded with scattered timber and oak thickets. Through the sweeping veils of windy rain, he made out the misted shapes of about twenty horses on the low ground to his right and well below. Bowie squatted down and dropped his saddle, scouring a palm over his stubbled jaw. He wet his thumb and tested the wind. Yeah — it would cut his scent at right angles away from them. But he'd have to work damned close before risking a cast, and it was a good hundred yards from the edge of timber to the herd.

11

Removing his catch rope from the saddle pommel, he went down the slope at a stiff-legged gait, clinging to the last trees. When he reached the open, he slowed and balled his body to a crouch as he moved carefully on, keeping the thickets between himself and the bunched horses. Patience. That was the watchword when you stalked horses. One thing, by God, he hadn't mustanged in the Mogollon country three years for nothing. But he'd have to shave his chances fine as froghair to get inside fair throwing range.

In a half hour Bowie reached the last thicket between him and the horses. They were still a hundred feet away. His throat tightened. Son of a bitch. Could he chance an approach across the open? He was close enough to make out a brand on the hips of several animals. Two linked circles. It meant nothing to him, except that this was owned stock, and the fact didn't deter him.

He'd begun easing to his feet, shaking out a loop of his coiled rope, when the horses started to shift away. Had they picked him up? He couldn't be sure; he would have to wait. He couldn't afford to miss his cast, not when he lacked any idea how far he was from human habitation.

Waiting, he felt his muscles start to quiver with tension and exhaustion and a gut-knotting hunger. Finally the horses halted and resumed their placid grazing.

Bowie continued to huddle on his heels, teeth

chattering, shoulders hunched against the slow rain. The mackinaw hung sacklike on his spare frame. Not a large man, he was stocky and hard. His callused, muscle-bunched hands, loosely closed around his coiled rope, made fists like knotty-oak dollops. His weathered features were blunt, not quite homely, with a truculent jaw sworled by thick black stubble and a craggy nose that had been broken a couple of times. His eyes were a darkish slate-gray and unpleasant; the rest of his face wasn't. His raven hair was streaked with gray at the temples and fantailed thickly over his ears and sheepskin collar. His appearance marked him as anywhere from forty to fifty; he was coming thirty-seven this winter. At least he reckoned so. Old Pap, a gaunt widower fighting all his days to wrest a living from red Georgia clay, had never kept clear track of his brood's ages or their doings: Bowie had been the youngest of seven.

Brooding in the rain, he had a brief set-to with his conscience. Not that he gave a hoot in hell about the letter of the law. Just that taking another man's horse violated a bedrock rule of his that was strictly personal. What the hell, though, it was just a borrow. He wouldn't keep his catch any longer than he had to.

The rain had nearly stopped, the thunder tapering to a sullen mutter, when the horses got restive again. They were pulling back this way. Bowie felt the heavy pound of his heart as he slowly rubbed his cold hands together. Close enough, he judged; it would have to be. He shucked off the bulky mackinaw and dropped it in the grass. Inching to his feet then, he shook out his rope and built a loop as he moved very slowly out to the open.

The horses gazed at him for a moment; men and ropes weren't new to them. A big buckskin gelding on the near flank of the bunch snorted and tossed his head. Bowie had already singled him out and he continued his bold approach, taking his time, talking softly. Suddenly the whole bunch wheeled and started to bolt.

Bowie lunged forward, at the same time whirling out his loop and making the throw, all in a motion. The noose spun smaller as it shot out; it was no wider than a barrel rim as it snapped over the buckskin's neck. Bowie pulled up short and set his heels as the animal's rush took up the slack. He hung doggedly on for long moments, coolly shifting to the horse's savage surgings as he bucked himself out. Finally it came to a lathered, heaving standstill.

Talking low, soothingly, Bowie walked toward the animal, coiling his rope. The buckskin stood motionless except for a quivering of muscles in his shoulders. "You'll be all right," Bowie told him. He laid his hand on the animal's neck, confident and friendly about it. "All right," he said.

Back in the timber, he bridled and saddled his catch while he gave the situation another gray study. Happen he were to confront the horse's owner, he didn't figure any explanation he might give would sound very damned convincing. He had a vivid memory of once seeing a horse thief kicking away his life from a cottonwood limb. Too chancy, lifting another man's horse and then riding into his place and explaining it was just a borrow. Best thing to do was just ride the buckskin south till he caught sight of the first habitation, then turn him loose and go in on foot.

The buckskin capered a little as he mounted, then quieted down. Bowie reined him downslope and southward, and let him run off his raw edge. As they passed through another belt of timber, the animal settled into a steady ground-eating pace. It was good to have horse-flesh under him again, but Bowie's mood merely notched upward from sour to less sour. He was still wet to the skin, his teeth rattling like casta-nets, and the wind cut his body like icy blades. When he came to the far fringe of the timber, he decided to make a stop and dry out as well as he could. The rain had quit completely, but from the sky's dismal look it could start up again any time. About the time you get dried out, he told himself dourly.

He halted by the timber's edge where trees would serve as a windbreak, then dismounted and tied the buckskin to a tree, making sure the tether rope was secure. Scouring up dry wood wasn't easy, and he was fifteen minutes assem-bling a small pile of branches. Half his matches missed fire before he coaxed a pyre of twigs into flame. It smoked like hell as he fed it with larger pieces, then cut some green limbs and rammed them into the ground by the fire to drape his clothes on.

He had removed his mackinaw and was on his knees propping it on the limbs when a rifle slug whanged off a knotty root about six yards away and sang away into the scanty brush.

Jesus God! Bowie froze where he was, on his knees. Then he moved only his head till he made out four riders. They'd topped the brow of a hill off right and maybe two hundred yards away, their yellow slickers shining wetly. The man who'd fired held his rifle pointed up; he shot into the air as the four put their horses down the hill. A shot unnecessarily warning Bowie to hold still.

They pulled up a few yards away and the man with the rifle piled off and walked over to the buckskin. He gazed at the brand, then at Bowie, slowly shaking his head. "Jesus. You are one dumb son of a bitch, ain't you? You long-loop a Chainlink horse, then fire up a smoke a blind man could spot across the county line."

Bowie said nothing. He felt the man's green stare size him up, his worn gear and tattered much-patched clothing, and he gave back a stony stare of his own. The man tramped over to stand above him. "You cocky goddam drifter. Talk up or I'll feed this rifle down your throat butt first."

He was squat as an ape, his arms long and

heavy, but didn't seem thick-bodied even in the bulky slicker. He moved with a trim rolling gait and his shoulders swelled with an oxlike power. His head fit the body: hair cropped close to a round brutish skull; features that were coarse and ruddy and underscored by a ruff of black beard. He was about thirty.

"Maybe that smoke says it, Brady."

Another rider had spoke up. Young and lean, he was dark-eyed, handsome in a Nordic way. But his straight black hair and coppery skin pointed to some blanket blood, and he sat his horse in a way that was definably Indian.

The apelike man's stare flicked to him. "How you mean?"

"Got a saddle, ain't he? Looks like he got set afoot and had to borrow a horse. If he didn't aim to keep him, why worry about making smoke?"

Brady gave a laugh and shake of his head. "I swear to Christ, Sully. Use them Injun eyes, why don't you? Look at this ugly-eyed bastard and his outfit. You can tell what he is plain as tits on a sow."

"Ho, then maybe he should say it," grinned another rider. He was a long and cat-flanked Mexican with a brown ax blade of a face. A knife scar hooked one corner of his yellow grin down to a gummy grimace. "What you say, Mester *chingado?* Will you tell us you don' steal the horse, hah?"

"Screw you, *chico*," Bowie said softly.

The fourth horseman gave a whickering laugh.

He looked enough like Brady that they were brothers for sure. Only he was younger and slighter and his eyes were a milky blue; he didn't look or sound too bright. "I guess he don't like your face, Trinidad," he said.

"Ai-yi! But he has *cojones,* this ugly one."

"I don't think he likes nobody's face, Joe-Bob," Brady said.

Without warning he tipped his rifle stock down and drove the butt savagely into Bowie's face. Slammed over on his back, Bowie lay dazed and unmoving. Sky and trees pinwheeled in his vision. It cleared slowly. He saw Brady loom above him.

"I don't like his face neither," Brady said. "I think I'll change it."

Bowie rolled his body sideways as the rifle stock came down. It missed his head, thudding on the wet loam. Then he was rolling hard into Brady's legs, grabbing blindly and clamping him around the knees. A strong heave and Brady, already off balance, was thrown heavily to the ground. Bowie floundered on top of him, pinning Brady's rifle between their bodies. He wrapped one arm around Brady's bullet head and drove three sledging blows into his face.

Trinidad wheeled his horse in close, bending low as he whipped back the skirt of his slicker. His arm pumped up, then down, his pistol barrel rapping across Bowie's skull. In the haze of red pain Bowie felt his hold loosen, and then Brady's savage heave flung him on his back.

18

Brady got to his feet, swaying as he clenched both fists around his rifle. "Damn cocky drifter," he said in a shaky, raging whisper.

"Ai-yi," Trinidad laughed. "He has eggs, this ugly one."

"Maybe we can lay a few more on him," Brady whispered. "Drag him, Trinidad."

"Ah, *amigo*. I don' know. Your old man, what will he say?"

"He don't need to know about it. Jesus, what do you want? We caught the bastard lifting a branded horse. That's good for a Dutch ride anyways." Brady's lips peeled off his teeth. "Had my way, I'd string him up right here."

"We ain't sure of nothing, Brady." Sully's voice was flat with disapproval.

"You still think it looks like a borrow? All right, let him say it. Go on, you damn ridgerunner. I want to hear you say it."

Bowie had struggled to his hands and knees. He stayed that way a moment, hanging his head, watching blood drip from his cut cheek onto the leaf loam. Slowly he raised his head till his eyes focused on Brady. "You shove it, mister," he whispered.

Brady smiled. "That answers it fine." He stepped back. "All right, Trinidad. Put a rope on him."

"I don't want no part of it," said Sully. He started to turn his mount.

"Sully." Brady's head tipped toward him. "You don't spill off about this, understand?"

19

The half-breed didn't answer. He loped his horse back toward the hilltop.

"I bet he tells Faye," grunted Trinidad. "That breed, he's in your old man's pocket."

"The hell with Faye." Brady's face was darkly flushed with anger. "Get to it."

"I don' know, *amigo.*"

"Goddammit, don't worry about Faye or the old man. Do as I say. I'll back you up."

Trinidad shrugged, then gigged his sorrel toward Bowie, shaking out a coil of his rope. Joe-Bob gave a high-pitched giggle. Trinidad was half smiling.

"Make him get up."

Brady took a long step and drove his boot into Bowie's side. He grunted and pulled away from the blow and Brady said savagely, "Stand up or you'll get another."

Bowie climbed to his feet, half paralyzed by the hurt of three blows. He hardly heard Brady's words; he only wanted to get his hands on him. He lurched painfully onto his feet and stumbled forward. Trinidad's noose shot out and brought him up short, pinning him around the chest and upper arms. The Mexican took a swift dally while his cow pony sidled against the slack. "She is a green rope," he grinned, "so you break in together, hey?"

He spurred away, yanking Bowie into a floundering run. He grabbed the rope in both hands and tried to brace, and was instantly jerked off his feet and scraped across the uneven ground for fifty bouncing, bruising yards. Then Trinidad reined up. Bowie lay face down in the wet grass, gagging. The raw pressure on his chest slacked a little. He looked up, his eyes swimming with pain.

Trinidad was chewing idly on a dead *cigarillo;* his gaze was sleepily amused. "Get up, tough one. That was only the little tickle."

Bowie got up on one knee, pausing to muster himself. He looked at the Mexican and at Brady and Joe-Bob watching from the grove's edge. His whole body twitched with raw hurt now, and he felt like retching. Instead he suddenly lifted his hands and whipped the rope off. He scrambled up and lurched in a blind stumbling run toward the Mexican, grabbing upward. Trinidad kneed his horse away, then planted a boot against Bowie's chest and shoved, knocking him backward in the grass.

Trinidad was no longer grinning. "*Jésus,*" he murmured. "You are like a mad dog. Don' you got no sense?"

Doggedly Bowie maneuvered onto his knees again, then to his feet. As Trinidad whirled out another deft loop, he flung up his arms. But the rope snared him once more; Trinidad sank his spurs. This time he dragged Bowie in a long circle, but before it was half completed, Bowie felt his consciousness ribboning off. He was aware of the jolting friction of earth under his body, but there was no more pain, no other sensation.

Suddenly he had stopped again. He knew that much. And then he knew a spreading circle of red-hot searing pain; it was eating into his chest. He tried to make a sound, but none came out. Splintered echoes of laughter rocked his ears. And that was all he knew.

CHAPTER TWO

"Nice work," Faye Nevers said. He glanced at Trinidad. "Nice rope work."

The Mexican shrugged, lazily grinning around his *cigarillo*. He sat his saddle with slack ease and locked Nevers's eyes with an insolent stare. "Brady say drag him."

"That's fine. Cyrus just might can your ass for it all the same."

Nevers swung off his short-coupled grullo and walked stiffly over to where the drifter lay sprawled by his dead fire. He gazed down at the unconscious man. The drifter's clothes were in dirty shreds; his face looked like raw meat. The front of his shirt had been burned away and red angry flesh showed through its blackened shreds.

"Dragged him over the fire, huh?"

Trinidad shrugged again. "I drag him off it too."

Nevers raised his sultry stare to Brady, who stood by grinning a little, his rifle hanging from one fist. "You did a job on him, didn't you?"

"After he stole a Chainlink horse."

"You know that, do you?" Nevers nodded at Sully, who was sitting his horse a few yards off. "He figures you're wrong. He's going to tell it to Cyrus that way."

"Sure. The old man's pet breed." Brady

looked at Sully and spat. "Pa's gone soft, Faye, and you know it. Leave it to him, all the long-looping trash in the country'll be cutting into our stock every time they take a mind. Somebody's got to show 'em the what-for of things."

"You can tell it to Cyrus." Nevers looked hard at Trinidad. "Cut a couple of poles and make a drag. We'll take him home."

Trinidad's grin faded and his gaze shifted to Brady.

"Don't look at him. I give you an order. Do it."

Brady tipped back his hat with his fist. "That's right, ain't it? Everyone takes your orders."

"That's what your pa says. You and Joe-Bob take 'em too. Any objections?"

"Why no," Brady said softly. "You're foreman, ain't you? But all my old man got to do is whisper cricket and you chirp."

Joe-Bob giggled foolishly.

Gazing at the two of them, Brady Trapp and his kid brother, Nevers felt a cold and savage disgust. The sons of Cyrus Trapp. But old Cyrus's blood had run thin as water in this pair: a thick-headed bully and a half-addled weakling.

Nevers said deliberately: "You know what, Brady? You wouldn't need to take my orders if you wasn't Cyrus's kin. Reason you wouldn't, I'd of kicked both your worthless asses off Chainlink long time ago. As it is, I'm supposed to keep you and the kid out of jackpots. That's an order too. I don't need to like it. It's just another job, even if it stinks."

Trinidad swung to the ground, pulled his Bowie knife from its sheath, walked to a straight sapling, and began hacking it down. Brady stood with his feet braced, the heavy blood crawling to his face. "The old man ain't going to be around forever, Faye," he said thickly. "You think about that."

"Now I'm scared," Nevers grunted. "Sully, give Trinidad a hand with that drag. You two," he added to Brady and Joe-Bob, "get over to Rock Spring and help Barney and Hilo comb the brush."

Brady climbed into his saddle and flung his mount around with a savage jerk of the reins. Joe-Bob stood where he was a slack-faced moment and then followed his brother as Brady kicked his animal into a run. Nevers knelt by the drifter and went over his body with deft hands, feeling for broken bones. Didn't seem to be any, though he looked more dead than alive. Just banged up all to hell. Great bruises were forming on his torso and the burn on his chest looked pretty bad.

Nevers stood up, gazing bleakly down at the man. Christ, what a scrubby-looking bastard. Brady was likely right about him. Not that it really mattered.

Faye Nevers looked bigger on his feet than on horseback. Tall, blond, roughhewn, he had the whittled hips of a horseman and the meaty, spreading shoulders of a smithy. His movements

25

were easy, leonine, long-muscled. His face had once been handsome; it was heavy and crooked-nosed and dimpled with scars, the face of a prize-ring pugilist or an inveterate barroom brawler. Nevers had been both. His eyes were the palest blue, remote and noncommittal.

Be a damned good thing to just leave this drifter where he was and say nothing. But Sully, who was intensely loyal to the old man, was bound to tell him what had happened, and Cyrus would be up in arms. He'd rant and roar anyway when he saw what had been done to the man, but this way Brady and Joe-Bob would catch the worst of it.

Hell of it was, Brady was right. How else could you protect all the drifting stock on a range this size? Hang 'em or drag 'em. Only way to put the fear of God into other sons of bitches with the same idea. Let the word get out they'd molly-coddled one horse thief, all the cross-dog scum in the country would regard Chainlink as easy pickings. Outfit like this one, built by a man who knew the uses of power, the man Cyrus Trapp had been, couldn't afford to soften its old free-wheeling ways as Cyrus seemed bound to do. Not and hold itself intact it couldn't.

Trinidad and Sully cut down three tall saplings and trimmed off the branches. Two saplings formed the parallel poles of the drag; the third was cut into three-foot lengths that were lashed between them. The ends were fastened to Sully's saddle. The men raised the limp, bat-

26

tered drifter onto the drag and tied him down with a few turns of rope.

They mounted up, and Nevers said: "Sully, I'll be riding in with you." He added to Trinidad: "You get over to Rock Spring and do what you're paid for."

"Sure, Faye. Uh, listen. You tell Old Man Trapp I just do what Brady say, huh?"

"All right. But you better read my sign straight from now on. You take orders from me, me alone. I hire and fire for this outfit and don't you forget it."

"Sure, sure —"

Damn that greaseball, Nevers thought, gazing after Trinidad as he rode gracefully away. He was a top hand, but you had to keep an iron rein on him. He'd been a *pistolero* in his younger days, and still had a taste for trouble that the cautions of middle age had only partly flagged down. Not that he was hard to handle except when he fell into company with the Trapp brothers.

Nevers's thoughts stayed sourly with that fact as he and Sully Calder rode southward, the burdened drag jouncing slowly behind them. If it wasn't one thing with that pair, it was something else. Brady had been raising hell of one sort or another since he was a kid; Cyrus had been bailing him out of one jam or another for years. Finally Cyrus had stuck both his sons on his cattle crew as punishment, and in hopes that working for wages would make them brace up. Did he really think that if Brady, at thirty-two, hadn't finished sowing his wild oats, he was likely to change? Joe-Bob, an addled twenty, merely followed his older brother's lead.

You couldn't blame the old man for being fed up, but it wasn't fair of him to expect his foreman to handle the affairs of a great ranch and assume responsibility for keeping his ne'er-do-well sons in line too. In his three years of ramrodding Chainlink, Nevers bitterly reflected, he'd welded its sprawling activities into a smooth-running operation. But how in hell could you keep the respect of crewmen who knew they'd be sent packing for pulling a fraction of the bullshit the boss's sons got away with?

Sully dryly broke the bleak run of his thoughts: "Going to cover yourself with Cyrus right away, eh? I'd say that's why you're helping me bring this fellow in."

"That's right," Nevers said bluntly. "You tell Cyrus how it happened and I'll be there to back you up. We'll scratch each other's backs."

Sully's eyes were darkly amused. "But you don't really reckon he was just borrowing that horse, do you?"

"Why, no." Nevers glanced at him with an open, contemptuous irony. "I'll leave it to you to help Cyrus uphold the goodness of man. Me, I just don't run against the boss's notions, no matter how damn fool they are."

Sully grinned. "Didn't figure you would. That's why I fetched you. Brady's right about one thing, though. He'll be heir to Chainlink someday — and it might not be far off. Kind of cutting your own throat, hard-mouthing him like you done."

Nevers's straight mouth tightened. "Maybe. Other hand, Cyrus could be around a long time yet. And I've taken all of Brady's smart-ass ways I can swallow."

"Too bad. When Brady takes over, you'll be out a place you was a long time working up to."

"What about you?" Nevers countered flatly. "You never really run afoul Brady before that I know of. Today you bucked flat against him, fetching me. Brady rides a grudge till kingdom come. Once he's in, where'll you and your sister be?"

Sully smiled wryly. "Out, I reckon. Not easy to think about that. Chainlink's the only place Tula and me can call home."

Nevers grunted. He remembered when Cyrus had taken in the two orphaned half-breeds many years ago. Their father, a hardscrabble rancher named Jim Calder who'd wed a Ute woman, had been a close friend of Cyrus Trapp's youth.

"Guess I'm like you," Sully said. "It came to where I had to stand up to Brady Trapp."

Sure, Nevers thought cynically, only for different reasons. Sully Calder was loyal to the man who had raised him and he shared Cyrus's new-found principles as well. Whereas Faye Nevers's star was to hold on with both fists to what he'd rightfully earned. He had climbed to the foremanship of Chainlink the hard way. His slum boyhood and years of oyster pirating in San Francisco Bay were long behind him. Fourteen years ago he'd started at Chainlink as a runny-nosed roustabout on one of Cyrus's chuck wagons. Eleven years later, when Cyrus's foreman had been killed in a town brawl, the man who was self-groomed to fill his boots had been Faye Nevers. He'd won every crumb, by God, that had fallen to his lot.

But Nevers had a gut-deep pride too; he wasn't taking any more of Brady Trapp's bullshit. Not even if it meant jeopardizing the only thing he cared for: the foremanship of Chainlink and the solid, hard-won respect that went with it. A bitter thing to think that he might have to start over one day. Hard too to think of ever leaving Chainlink. The place had become like a part of him, blood and bone.

And there was another reason, one he confided only to himself. There was Adah. The beautiful second wife whom Cyrus Trapp had brought to Chainlink six months ago, the wife less than half his age.

Adah Trapp. As beautiful and unapproachable as an iceberg. A Lady Priss-pants if he'd ever seen one: a fitting mate for an old man. But there was bitter self-mockery in Nevers's thought. He couldn't explain why; he only knew that no woman he'd ever known, and he'd known many, had affected him the way Adah Trapp did. He'd spent endless hours puzzling on why the sight of her made him go hollow-bellied and pulse-heavy.

And wondering what the hell he could do about it.

Bowie nearly came to four or five times in the next few hours, but each time the pain swept him away and he mercifully blanked out. He was aware of faces, of voices, of the inside of a room, but none of it made any sense. Finally he slept.

When he came to again, he was clear-headed. The room held steady in his vision as he lay still and let his gaze touch everything in it. Mortar-chinked log walls darkened with age and brightened by a few old calendars featuring Currier & Ives lithographs. A battered commode with a lamp on it. The flame was turned low, the room shadow-filled; the single window was a dark square. It was night. And he was on his back in a big brass-framed bedstead with a bright-checked quilt pulled to his neck.

He moved one arm. Jesus God! The movement showered echoes of pain through his body. Most of it felt like the blunt throbbing of heavy bruises. Except where pain centered like a live coal on his chest. And his head, which felt as if an ax had been sunk into it.

He grimaced, trying to remember.

Those men. Being dragged. His mind tightened around the memory with a raw, humiliated hatred. Those sons of bitches. Had they brought him to . . . wherever he was? Didn't make much sense, considering what they'd done.

31

Well, by God. Maybe he could find a few answers. Shudderingly he eased to a sitting position; every hurt blazed to agonizing life. He felt like vomiting; he sat quietly till the feeling passed. Christ. Ignoring the savage slugging in his skull, he threw off the blankets and slowly swung his legs to the floor. He was wearing a clean suit of baggy flannel underwear, not his own. He saw his saddle and other gear on the floor by a wall. Moving with infinite care, he got to his feet, stood swaying a moment as he crowded back the surging waves of dizziness, then moved to the commode and the scroll-framed mirror on the wall behind it.

The bastards had done a real job on him, all right. His face was scabbed with cuts and purpled with bruises; his jaw was swollen lopsidedly, one eye nearly shut. He didn't reckon the rest of him looked any better. But his chest. Christ, what had happened there? He undid the underwear buttons and saw a bandage with a flat bulge of poultice underneath. He touched it and shuddered at the raw swell of pain. A burn? The Mexican must have dragged him across his own fire.

A heavy pulse began to beat in Bowie's neck as he stared at his battered reflection. His swollen jaw knotted so tight that he winced. The rage he felt was hot, feral, unreasoning. Somebody was going to pay for this. Hobbling on bare feet to the window, he peered out. Faint outlines of ranch buildings in the darkness. Couldn't tell much except that this was a second-story window. So he'd go out another way.

First thing was to find his goddam clothes. Take them at gunpoint if he had to. He scanned his saddle plunder; everything was here but his rifle. Smart bastards. The blind fury curdling in him colored his thoughts to an unheeding violence. All right — all right. Find a gun. Then, by God.

He padded over to the door, palmed it softly open, and stepped out onto a wide landing. He saw a railed stairwell with lamplight shafting from downstairs. Faint voices drifted from below. Doors along the wall, probably bedchambers, and it must be early in the evening yet. He'd search for a gun. Matches. He'd need matches. A search of his saddlebags turned some up. Silently he tried the first door to his left, grimaced as he got a whiff of female cologne, and closed it. The next room was tenanted by somebody who worked cattle; he struck a match and saw a Spencer rifle mounted on wall pegs. He found a box of .54 cartridges in a drawer of the commode. He slid a shell in the breech and filled the Spencer's loading tube, then eased out to the stairway.

There he paused, listening to the voices from below, trying to single them out. A woman's. Several men's. And one throaty, surly voice that made hair prickle at the back of his neck. *Brady.* His hand clenched in savage reflex around the rifle.

33

Bowie went down the steep rises in silence. He was sweating profusely, his teeth set against pain, as he reached the bottom of the stairs. He stood in a short shadowy corridor that ended in a doorway on either end. He promptly guessed that the closed door on his right led to the kitchen. The ajar one on his left opened on the dining room. He could only see one end of it from here, but the voices coming from it, along with a tinkle of china and utensils, indicated that the people were at supper.

". . . time you'd have hung that sort of long-looping trash from a tree," Brady was saying sullenly.

"Times change," another voice rumbled. An older man's voice, deep and commanding. "In my time there wasn't no law but what a man made for himself. I burned plenty powder making it stick. But them days is over. We're in a county now, we got elected officials. Man's got a complaint, he takes it to a sheriff. That's as it should be."

"Hell!" Brady said hotly. "That's the half of it — you changed too, don't tell me you ain't, you talk like —"

"You shut your mouth. Hear me out. I won't say this again. I'm the man I always been. But I made all the mistakes I mean to. There's a couple of my prime ones sitting at this table." A flat pause broken by Joe-Bob's quiet titter. The old man's voice went on, softly hard and unrelenting. "You ain't the man I was, Brady. You never will be. You couldn't build in a hundred years what I built in twenty. You'll never need to; I seen to that. But try to play the game like I played it, you'll lose it all."

Bowie edged noiselessly forward till he could see into the room. Brady was starting up from his chair; he crumpled his napkin and threw it on his plate. "All right, by God!" he shouted. "All right, you can —"

His lifting glance froze on the doorway where Bowie stood, lank and wiry in the loose underwear. He let out a whoop. "I'll be goddamned! Look at —"

He broke off, for Bowie was bringing the rifle up from his side. He thumbed back the hammer and pulled the trigger. A shard of brittle wood exploded from a wall log at Brady's back and less than a foot from his right arm. The roar of the shot was deafening in the room.

The woman screamed.

"Funny, wasn't it?" Bowie said.

He cocked the Spencer again.

Joe-Bob leaped to his feet, his chair crashing over. He gaped stupidly and made no other move. Brady hung against the table, both hands on it, his black-bearded jaw sagging. Bowie's glance moved across the damask-covered table. He barely looked at the woman; her face was wide-eyed and colorless. The fourth person at the table climbed slowly to his feet.

He was as big as his voice, a huge-boned, brown-faced man of about sixty. The years had been kind to him; his close-cropped chestnut hair and beard held only a few strands of gray. He moved as easily and powerfully as a man twenty years younger. His eyes were still eagle fierce, though a pair of spectacles rested on his beak of a nose. They didn't dim his solid presence; his face held neither surprise nor anger.

"All right, son," he said quietly. "You done your little bit of play-acting. I'm Cyrus Trapp. You got some'at to say, you say it to me."

Bowie grinned mirthlessly. "Cyrus Trapp don't mean a goddam thing to me, mister."

The woman gave a little whispered cry.

"Don't be alarmed, Adah honey," Trapp said. He patted her shoulder. "He is just shooting at walls."

"So far," Bowie said.

Cyrus Trapp shook his head. "They said you was feisty as hell. But you got a mote of sense too or you'd of bored Brady straight off. You ain't here for that."

Bowie nodded. "So far you ain't wrong. I want my clothes first. Then I'll tell you what next."

"Maybe you better say it now."

"All right. I'm going to wrap this gun around Brady's skull. Then I'm —"

A movement of the woman's eyes, then Joe-Bob's, warned him. He started to wheel around, but too late. Somebody had come silently up behind him and now he threw his arms around Bowie's torso, pinning his arms. Bowie heaved and struggled. Pointed up in his fists, the Spencer bellowed again; the bullet crashed into the ceiling.

Adah screeched again. Bowie ducked his head, then slammed it backward in the unseen man's face. He gave a pained yell and his hold loosened. Bowie drove a savage elbow into his ribs and knocked him away.

Brady was already coming fast around the table, was almost on him, and Bowie whipped the rifle up. The butt of the stock crunched against Brady's face and sent him slamming back against the wall. Bowie swung on Cyrus, who was coming at him from the other side. In the same instant the man behind him, recovering, wrapped an arm around Bowie's neck and rammed a knee in his back, arching him off balance.

Cyrus wrested the Spencer from Bowie's grasp and moved back, saying, "All right, Sully. Leave go of him."

Freed, Bowie stumbled against the table and grabbed at it for support. He glared at the old man, but the soreness of his body and the rifle in Cyrus's hands banked the unrelieved anger in him. He swung a glance on Brady, who was still sagging dazedly against the wall, fingering his split mouth. Blood funneled off the tip of his beard and splashed on his white shirt.

"How's your lip?" Bowie asked.

With a snarl Brady pushed away from the wall and started for him, but Cyrus roared, "That's enough, Brady!" He gave Bowie a prod with the rifle muzzle. "You sit down. Sit, I said!"

Bowie dropped into a chair, leaning his elbows on the table and cupping a hand to his aching head. He looked at Sully, who was holding a bandanna to his bleeding nose and, surprisingly, chuckling a little. "I told you he was a real hardnose, Cyrus. You should of put a guard on him."

Cyrus grunted. "What brought you from the bunkhouse so providentially?"

"Oh, I'd just come into the kitchen to have a few words with Tula. Overheard the talk in here." Sully grinned. "Glad I did, even if it saved Brady a busted head. Or did it?"

"That's funny, breed, funny as hell," Brady husked. His green eyes blinked hatred at Bowie. "Told you it was a mistake, Pa. Taking him into the house. I told you."

"Could be," Cyrus said dryly, "that you made the first mistake, having him dragged."

"Then I'll make it right." Brady's voice seethed with rage. "Turn the son of a bitch over to me now. I'll run his ass clear across the county line."

"Boy, you been warned to curb your immoderate language under this roof. Do I got to tell you again?"

"But *cripes,* Pa! You keep him here, he could murder us all in our sleep!"

"Not you, Junior," Bowie said, his voice soft and jeering. "I'll just pull down your drawers and spank your pink bottom for saying bad words."

There was raw murder in Brady's face. He stood flexing and unflexing his fists, then suddenly turned and tramped through an archway that opened on the adjoining parlor. He went out the front door, slamming it behind him. Sully was shaking with noiseless laughter. A girl had come from the kitchen, and as she moved up beside Sully, he dropped an arm around her shoulders. She was a lot smaller than he, but it was plain they were brother and sister.

Adah said faintly, "Tula. Will you bring my smelling salts, please?"

"Yes, ma'am." The girl went out, her steps going briskly up the stairs.

The front door opened; a big blond man stepped into the parlor. He paused, briefly taking in the scene. His eyes were as impersonal as a snake's. "Anything wrong? Heard a couple of shots and just saw Brady come stomping out —"

"All's under control, Faye," Cyrus said. "But you might dispatch one of the boys over here. Tell him to bring his hogleg. I think we'll put a guard by our drifter man's door tonight."

Faye nodded. "I'll send Barney." He went out.

Bowie rubbed his head. It was pounding unmercifully; his eyes were starting to blur. His muscles felt rubbery with aching exhaustion. "Jus' gimme my clothes," he muttered. "Don' wanta stay here."

"Why, son," Cyrus said dryly, "I make it you are feverish and not thinking straight. You better lay over tonight. Anyway you got no horse."

"I figure I earned the buckskin."

Sully laughed. "No end to his vinegar, is there? Maybe he's right, Cyrus."

Cyrus twitched a brief smile. "That's as may be. Sheriff might reason otherwise."

Bowie dropped the hand from his forehead and glowered at him. "That's why you're holding me, ain't it?"

"You sleep on the thought. We'll talk when you got that fever damped some. That sandy temper of yours too. You are starting to rub mine just a mite thin, son."

CHAPTER THREE

He was stiff and still sore as hell when he woke next morning, but his headache had subsided to a tolerable throb and he was ravenously hungry. A glance through the window told him the sun was midmorning high. The sky was a new-scrubbed blue; the day looked crisp and pleasant. Easing himself gingerly upright in bed, he saw fresh clothes, not his own, hung on the back of a chair. His own runover boots stood beside it. Bowie hobbled over to the door and opened it a crack. That damn guard was gone. Maybe he could clear out of here now. Then he uneasily remembered that his next move depended on Cyrus Trapp's whim. Even could he sneak out, Trapp could set the law on his trail. Hell!

Bowie pulled on the well-worn but clean shirt and pants and socks. The clothes hung sacklike on his gaunt frame, so oversize that he judged they were Cyrus Trapp's own. A pitcher, wash basin, and shaving gear had been set out on the commode. Damn considerate, he thought dourly. He didn't know if he could pare the wiry scrub off his raw face, but he felt mean enough to try. He whipped up a lather in the shaving mug and slapped it on his beard.

Waiting for the soap to soften his whiskers, Bowie tramped to the window and stared out. Chainlink headquarters was quite a layout, he had to admit. The intricate but well-ordered complex of sheds, wagon sheds, stables, horse troughs, bunkhouse, cookshack, smithy, smokehouse, storage cribs, corrals, and cattle pens was spread across a deep valley flat between timber hills. A hell of a lot for one man to lay claim to, along with a parcel of range that must extend far into the foothills he'd covered yesterday. Studying the shape of the country from this north window, Bowie knew the headquarters was considerably south of where he'd been dragged yesterday.

Finished stropping the razor, he carefully attacked his beard, wincing and swearing. He hadn't noticed before that the worst of his facial cuts had been sewed up with small neat stitches. Not that it mattered a hell of a lot; his hide already bore worse scars than any Trinidad's dragging was like to leave. The poultices had nicely relieved the excruciating burn on his chest.

Stiff-legged, he descended to the dining room. Cyrus Trapp sat alone at the head of the table, eating his eggs while he peered through his spectacles at a frayed newspaper. "Morning, son. You don't look half as ugly without the fur. Sit yourself and eat. My boys are already up and out, and my wife sleeps late. Won't nobody bother us."

Bowie remained standing in the doorway. "You wanted to talk."

"That can wait. Fill your belly first. See a night's sleep didn't wear off none of your bark."

42

"Too damn bad, ain't it?"

Bowie seated himself at the foot of the table, turned over his face-down plate, and began loading it from the platter of ham and eggs. He attacked the food with a famished concentration and in silence. Cyrus said nothing until he'd finished and had washed the meal down with black coffee. Standing up then and chucking his napkin on the table, Cyrus said: "Come along. We'll palaver in the parlor."

As they entered the big sitting room, Bowie gave it an indifferent glance, but he was impressed. This was a man's room for sure. The west wall was graced by the biggest fireplace he'd ever seen, solidly built of soot-seasoned field stones. The oaken ceiling beams were polished by smoke and age to a rich darkness. The furniture was old and heavy, horsehair sofas and hand-carved armchairs scattered casually around the room, as were the thick-weave Indian blankets that served as rugs. The walls were hung with trophy heads of elk, antelope, and bighorn, along with flintlock rifles and muskets, old pistols and cutlasses, and a collection of Indian weapons. As he seated himself on the edge of the least comfortable-looking chair, Bowie fleetingly reflected that the haughty-looking woman called Adah wasn't Trapp's daughter after all. His wife. Huh. Pretty recent union, seemed like. She sure-hell hadn't yet dented the solid masculinity of this place.

Cyrus settled into an armchair with a grunt.

43

"Now. You want to find me a reason I shouldn't turn you over to Sheriff Beamis?"

"Might be more interesting to let your cub kick my ass across the county line like he wants. Let him try."

Cyrus took a cigar from his pocket and eyed it almost with distaste. "All right, play it hardnosed. I can ride it out a little longer. Just for the hell of it, son, why don't you tell me the truth? Sully said he figured you just borrowed the buckskin. But you wouldn't answer up when Brady put the question."

"I didn't like how he asked it."

"Make a difference if he'd asked polite?"

"I'll tell you this," Bowie said flatly. "It would of made no goddam difference to Junior how I answered."

Cyrus sighed and nodded. "Well, I can't fault the truth in that — mind saying your name? You got mine."

"Bowie Candler."

"All right, Candler. You seem to understand tit for tat. You square with me, I'll square with you. Fair enough?"

Bowie shrugged.

"Goddammit, yes or no?"

"All right."

The chair creaked as Cyrus canted his weight forward. "Here's my side. I'd of heard you out and decided whether I believed you. Happen I didn't, I'd never drag a man on a rope or roast him on a fire. Time was I might of hanged you.

But that's long past. Now I'd turn you over to Beamis. Still might if your story don't ring true. You want to tell it?"

"Ain't much to tell. Lion run my horse off night before last. I was afoot, wet, half-froze, and that saddle was damn heavy." Bowie paused. "I never lifted horseflesh before, but I didn't feel like drawing no distinctions. Meant to turn him loose soon as I raised a road or a ranch. That's all."

Cyrus rose and walked to a window, chewing his cigar. He faced out across his valley and said without turning: "Takes a lot to build up a place like this, Candler. Lot of years, lot of sweat, some blood. Takes a tough son of a bitch to do it, which I was. Still am. Brady don't think so. He's never understood there's different kinds of strength. Takes the biggest kind of guts to take a chance on people. He's never understood that either."

Cyrus half turned from the window, rubbing a slablike hand over his face. Then he pressed the hand tight against his temple. His eyes were squinted shut; his gritted jaw bulged against his beard.

"What's wrong?"

"Nothing," Cyrus said curtly. "Not a goddam thing." He dropped the hand and strode back to his chair. "I'll take your word, Candler. You still lifted that buckskin, borrow or not."

"So it's the sheriff."

"Christ, you're thick-headed," Cyrus said irritably. "I could hand you to Beamis without pumping you first. What I propose is to let you work out the buckskin's price if you're willing. If you ain't, you can walk out of here and straight to hell, for all I care. We're about to begin fall roundup and I need another hand. What about it?"

"I get to keep the buckskin?"

"Jesus." Cyrus shook his head, slowly and wonderingly. "I just said as much, didn't I? Maybe cow work's too complicated for you."

"I handled plenty before." Bowie met his wickedly measuring stare with one in kind. "You got a damn salty tongue yourself, mister."

"I can afford one." Cyrus was pressing his temple again, but the squinch of pain in his eyes didn't soften. "I can back it. Back it one helluva lot handier than any out-at-the-heels pilgrim can."

Bowie rubbed a hand over his mouth to hide the grin suddenly jerking at one corner of it. "Hope your grub's easier to swallow than you are."

"You'll find out. How you like them clothes?"

"Since you ask, they don't suit me worth a goddam."

"That's all right. You'll appreciate 'em better when you've worked out their price too."

"Like hell I will," Bowie said promptly, flatly. "I paid for the borrow of that horse by getting dragged. That squares it. But Junior ruined my duds too, and goddamned if I'll pay a plugged

46

penny for your cast-offs."

Cyrus merely nodded, mild again. "All right. Just one more thing, Candler. You got any sand left in your craw concerning my son, get it spit out."

Bowie thought it over, then nodded. "That's fair. But I won't take no goddam rawhiding off him. You tell him."

"He'll get the word. Faye Nevers, he's my foreman, has got orders to put his heel on Brady any way need be." As if the admission shamed him, Cyrus got abruptly to his feet. "Fetch your plunder to the bunkhouse. Rest up all you can today. Last chance you'll get to while you're eating Chainlink grub."

"Honest to God, Pa," Brady said savagely. "I don't understand you at all! First you let that mangy drifter con you with a goddam lie, then you hire him on the crew. It's like patting a thief on the back because he lifted your poke."

"That'll do," Cyrus said curtly. "I don't want to hear no more on it. And you don't raise any more ruction with Candler, hear me? He's on, and that's an end of it."

Faye Nevers sat with elbows braced on the table, revolving his coffee cup between his palms. A faint frown creased his heavy face. Cyrus had invited him for supper so they could discuss plans for the roundup, but the whole meal had been another session of bickering between Cyrus and his older son. Adah sat picking at her food, mouth pursed with disapproval. Joe-Bob just listened and grinned. Cyrus slanted a dry glance at Nevers.

"What's sitting in your craw, Faye? Speak up."

Nevers set his cup down. "You kind of closed the subject."

"Never mind. Say it."

"We got a full crew for roundup. We don't need this Candler, even if he wasn't a horse thief. All right, you believe his story. But he's a hard-nose, you seen it for yourself. Man like that on the crew'll make trouble."

Brady thumped his fist on the table. "There, your foreman said it —"

"Shut up," Cyrus said, not looking at him. "Go on, Faye."

"It's been my understanding that I do the hiring and firing for Chainlink. If that's changed, I'd like to hear it said."

"You'll hear it said when I change it. I been dealing with men all my life, Faye. If I'd made many wrong guesses, I'd not be alive to tell you. All right, I'm taking Candler on faith. If I stretched our understanding, call it an old man's whim. Give him a chance. If he's troublesome, let him go. It's still up to you."

Nevers gave a noncommittal nod. "Fair, I reckon."

Brady scraped back his chair and stood up, muttering, "Jesus. Come on, kid."

"Just a minute. Where you off to?"

"The bunkhouse." Brady gave his father a

48

hostile grin. "For a turn of cards. *That* all right?"

"You mind what I said about Candler."

Brady and Joe-Bob went out; the door slammed. Cyrus sighed, took out his daily cigar, now chewed almost to a stub, and set it in a corner of his mastiff jaws. "I hope them poker games are kept low stake."

Nevers smiled. "Only kind the boys can afford. You know how it gets after payday. Everyone's wages is pretty much common property, way it changes hands. One good night in town and it's all blowed anyway."

Cyrus grunted. "Just so long as Brady blows his share on redeye and crib girls."

"Cyrus, please." Adah's face had pinkened; her eyes were lowered.

"Sorry, honey. I forgot. You don't know about that."

"About what?"

"Couple years ago, Brady run up some heavy debts at the gaming tables over in Saltville. I paid up his score under the strict condition that his big-gambler days were over. He has got to confine his bellystripping to the bunkhouse. So far's I know, he has."

Nevers sipped his cold coffee to hide his ironic twist of mouth. He knew that three months ago, Brady had again begun frequenting Lucky Jack's casino in Saltville. Seemed a fair bet that by now the owner held a bundle of Brady's IOU's. In his gambling, as in most things, Brady was plunging and incautious, too stubborn to learn better, too

49

hot-headed to give a rip about the consequences. Nevers's lips curled wryly. Cyrus knew men, but that trusting nature of his was a blind spot. Bred by the code of his generation of cattlemen, the iron code that a man's handshake was his bond, he expected to be dealt with in kind. Damned if I'm sticking my neck out, Nevers thought. Leave him find out in his own time.

When Tula had finished clearing the table and Adah had retired to the parlor to pore over the latest *Century Magazine*, Cyrus brought paper and pencil to the table. He and Nevers spent the next hour going over details for the big roundup. It would involve roughly fifty square miles of valley and foothill country and all the cattle outfits within that range. The meeting place for its northern division would be the valley of the Oro River along Chainlink's east boundary. Some two hundred men and fifteen hundred horses would be divided between a half-dozen captains and their wagons, and they would work the country in the pattern of previous roundups. As foreman for one of the biggest outfits, Nevers would be a wagon captain, with the job of representing and cutting for all brands in the division.

"That's about it," Cyrus said finally. "Gonzales has laid in plenty of supplies and his wagons are loaded and ready to roll. You'll start out at daybreak tomorrow."

"That sounds like you won't be coming along."

Cyrus pursed his mouth. "I'll be along in a

50

couple days. You'll have letters of authorization from me and our ten-cow neighbors that ain't sending reps. That ought to satisfy the inspectors from the stock associations. I — have got a few things to take care of here. Then I'll be along."

Nevers's eyes narrowed; his attention sharpened. It wasn't like Cyrus to pass up the neighborly hurly-burly of a roundup. Not like him to be vague about reasons either. Nevers was debating whether to put the question to him when he noted a jerking, painful squint in Cyrus's eyes. A condition he'd noticed before, more frequently in the last week or so. One moment Cyrus seemed clear-eyed and healthy as a bull; the next, he was blinking and wincing as if against some pain that was intolerable. His big hand came up to his temple and began to slowly massage it.

Nevers decided to state it flat out. "Look, if it's none of my business, say so. I been wondering what the trouble is."

Cyrus let the hand fall. "No damn trouble at all."

"Sorry."

"Hell, it's nothing. Get these headaches now and again. Come and go. Need new spectacles is all." Cyrus leaned suddenly hard against the table, his elbow slamming down. His broad face twitched and twisted against an invisible agony. "Christ," he whispered. "Christ!"

"Listen —" Nevers started to his feet. "What's ailing you?"

51

"Nothing," Cyrus said hoarsely. His shaggy head was bent, both hands cradling it. "Leave it be —"

Nevers skirted the table and went to the archway. "Mrs. Trapp, you better come in here."

Adah rose from the settee and came quickly into the dining room. "Cyrus — Cyrus, not again."

He gave a jerky nod, not raising his head. "Lea' me be. All right in a minute."

She laid her hands on his shoulders. "Please, dear, come to bed. You don't want to fall down as you did . . . once before. Let me help you."

Cyrus lowered his hands, slowly and heavily nodding. "All right." His face was a sweaty gray; his gaze shifting to Nevers was dull with pain. "Faye, you don't tell a soul about this. Not a soul."

"I won't," Nevers said. "Here, I'll lend a hand."

Between them, Adah and Nevers helped Cyrus to his feet. He was as unsteady as a year-old baby, his eyes blind and unfocused. Nevers took the bulk of Cyrus's weight against his own shoulder as they maneuvered the big man up the stairs to his room. They lowered him onto the bed. Nevers tasted the strangeness of seeing a man he had always thought of as a monument, invincible to wear and time, helpless as a kitten.

"Maybe we better send to Saltville for Doc Rawls. If —"

"No!" Cyrus snarled the word, hands pressed over his eyes. "No doctor. Goddammit, Faye, mind what I told you."

"All right. Take it easy. Couple blasts of home-grown painkiller might help —"

"You know I can't take any booze."

"Right," Nevers said softly. "I forgot."

Adah touched his arm. He nodded and followed her out the door, gently closing it as a muffled groan exploded from Cyrus. They went down the stairs; Adah halted by the archway. Her face was pale and unreadable. Almost. She's scared, he thought.

"It's happened before, eh?"

"Twice — this badly, I mean. Once last week. Again two nights ago. But the headaches — he's been having them off and on for nearly two months. I've urged him to see Dr. Rawls, but —" Her shoulders lifted and settled.

"Uh-uh. He wouldn't, not Cyrus."

She shook her head; a stain of worry darkened her eyes. "I don't know . . . what I can do. Several times — in the night — I've lain awake in the next room listening to him toss and groan. Sometimes for hours. But he refuses even to discuss it. I fear the worst, Mr. Nevers."

So Cyrus and his bride didn't share the same bed. Nevers had suspected as much from his sight of Cyrus's room. He remembered the same rickety old bedstead and spartan furnishings from years back. It might have been consideration for Adah, as his affliction had grown worse, that had caused Cyrus to move back into his former room. All the same, Nevers felt a burning curiosity.

It made him more sharply aware of the woman's nearness. The familiar surge of rampant feeling boiled into his guts; he had difficulty holding his expression still and just faintly concerned. The problem had begun when Cyrus had brought his bride to Chainlink six months ago.

Cyrus Trapp's remarriage after nineteen years as a widower had come as a complete surprise to everyone, even his sons. As it turned out, he'd been a frequent visitor at Adah Landry's home in Denver for many years. Adah's father, also a widower, had been one of Cyrus's oldest friends. After an accident had left him crippled and half paralyzed, Adah had devoted her youth to caring for him. Apparently they'd lived pretty much from hand to mouth; though Cyrus had never said so, Nevers had gathered that he'd helped the Landrys out more than once, and very likely he'd footed the bill for Adah's education at an excellent boarding school. Cyrus's forceful generosity was legend; he'd practically belabor a friend in need to accept his bounty. Adah had been a spinsterish twenty-six when her father had died two years ago — and Cyrus had continued his regular calls.

The affection between them was genuine enough. But romantic? Nevers couldn't see it. For all the difference in their ages, of course,

Cyrus was still a vital, far-from-doddering man; Adah was a thoroughly mature woman. There had to be that much. Cyrus had been lonely too, hungry for a familial warmth he'd never found with his sons. Nevers summed up Adah's position with a sardonic judgment. She'd been grateful. Also destitute. And she'd wanted another father.

But Jesus, what a waste. A woman like this thrown away on an old man. When Cyrus was seventy, she'd still have it all. The chiseled beauty of a face with tantalizing planes and tilts that reminded Nevers of the Oriental girls he'd known in his West Coast youth. Eyes of a lovely sharp-colored turquoise under delicately winged brows. Skin like pale satin and black hair that glistened like fresh tar in its prim chignon. The proper high-necked dresses she always wore couldn't do justice to her erect slim full-breasted figure. Gentle, genteel, quiet: that was Adah. The Adah everyone saw. But a woman couldn't look like her and not have a fierce womanliness waiting to blossom just under the surface. . . .

She was gazing at a wall, and now her eyes moved back to his face. "What did Cyrus mean — that remark about booze? I know he never drinks, but —"

"Thought you knew. Reckon he'd of told you if the matter ever came up. He can't take the stuff. Never could."

"I don't understand."

"All I know is what he told me once. Little bit

55

of liquor, enough to warm another man's innards, does something to Cyrus — sends him off his head, he told me. He never takes a drink because he don't dare to."

"Oh," she said softly. "I had no idea."

Momentarily Nevers debated whether to add what else Cyrus had told him. That only after he'd once beaten a man to death with his fists while drunk had he taken a vow never to touch liquor again. No — that wasn't for him to say.

"Is there anything else I can do?"

"I'm afraid not." She bit her lip gently. "If you could persuade him to see a doctor — but if he won't listen to me, will he to you?"

Nevers shook his head soberly.

Again he held a cool mask over the quick sensuous turn of his thoughts. What would she do if he touched her? Scream? Slap him? He felt a reckless amusement, toying with the possibility.

Her eyes seemed to dilate darkly as they met his now. But that was all. Maybe he'd imagined it.

"Good night, Mrs. Trapp."

"Good night."

Nevers felt a gnawing uneasiness as he tramped through the darkness toward the bunkhouse. Just how serious was Cyrus's condition? What did it mean for Chainlink — for his own future here? But these speculations ebbed behind the excitement still thrumming in his veins.

Adah. Prissy Adah. He tried to mock her in his thoughts. But damn it, damn it to hell, he was only mocking himself. . . .

CHAPTER FOUR

The work was hard and the hours long. Starting in the foothill country below the Elks, the northern division of the roundup pushed southward along the great Oro valley. Ahead of the wagons, outriders fanned out in wide circles, pushing all the cattle they picked up down toward the valley flats where the roundup crews would take them over. On the morning following each day's drive, all the local cattle were cut from the gather and turned loose. The strays were headed into a separate herd, which was driven along at a distance from the wagons. Actually six different roundups were carried on at the same time across the valley, with six different crews each assigned to a wagon and a captain. Every night the separate details met up with their wagons at a rendezvous point down river.

It was familiar work to Bowie, assigned as an outrider to Faye Nevers's wagon. Work he didn't mind as much as he did the miserable weather that had plagued the roundup from the first day. Every time it seemed to be letting up some, mare's tails of storm would curve out of the dismal stewing sky above the northern Elks. In an hour or so the prairie hills would be enveloped in a powdery murk of drizzle that was halfway between fog and rain. It wasn't as bad as a good honest storm; it was worse. Gray and depressing, the damp eating more into a man's disposition than into his slicker-clad body.

Bowie's mood wasn't improved by having young Sully Calder in his vicinity most of the time. He had the idea that Sully was deliberately hanging close, and the half-breed's undented cheerfulness fed his irritation. He remembered what Trinidad had said to Brady about Sully being "in your old man's pocket."

Finally he said bluntly to Sully: "Trapp figure I need a wet nurse?"

"Nope," said Sully, unfazed. "A watchdog. Cyrus dropped a word to Nevers, and the word is I am to stick close to you."

"They figure I can run off this whole damn herd?"

"You sound mean enough to try," Sully chuckled. "Hell, they're only curious how you'll work out. I'll be asked about you. Nothing to get sweated over." He added thoughtfully, "Cyrus seems to of taken a personal interest in you."

"What the hell for?"

"You'd have to ask him."

"I wouldn't ask that crusty old fart the time of day."

They were trailing in the drag of the day's gather, and now Sully reined over close to his stirrup and said: "Listen, Candler." He didn't sound angry, only positive. "You're about as sour a pilgrim as I ever butted against. Maybe you got reason to be, I wouldn't know. But don't make no mistake about Cyrus Trapp. All right, times he's like a Dutch uncle, other times he gets under your saddle like a gallsore. But rain or shine, he's the best man I ever knew. Best you're ever like to meet."

"Yeah? What's he done for you?"

"Everything," Sully said flatly. They jogged along in silence for a minute, and then he said: "I was fifteen year old, Tula just twelve, when our folks died. Our ma was one of a big band of Utes that used to summer in the high country. Pa had a one-loop spread west of here and my ma's relatives used to camp in our back yard half the year round. Pa was practically the only white man we ever seen. Tula and me grew up with our Ute cousins, learning their ways, talking their tongue. I used to hunt and fish with my full-blood kin." His lips smiled with memory. "It was a great life."

"Sounds like it," Bowie said, and meant it.

"Yeah. What ended it, the pox hit that summer and just about wiped out the band. Our ma was one of the first to go. Tula and me only come down with light attacks. Our white blood, I reckon. Anyway Ma's death hit Pa pretty hard. He got drunk in Saltville and was killed in a shooting scrape. We never did get the way of it straight. Cyrus took us kids in. Raised us like his own. Sent Tula away to school; she just returned a few months back. Me, I had a choice as to the same, but was satisfied with things way they was."

"You might's well be." Bowie swiveled a

glance at him. "You two ain't aught but servants for the Trapps. Pretty damn beholden, ain't you?"

Sully smiled, shaking his head. "You just naturally like to prod a man, don't you? I'm doing what I choose, Candler. As for Tula, what better you think a half-blood girl will find any other place?"

Bowie shrugged. "I ain't spent a lot of time this far north. A breed don't amount to much down by the border."

"He don't amount to much up here either. Anyway Chainlink is our home, Tula's and mine. Reckon you wouldn't understand that."

Bowie didn't consider that worth affirming.

It was late in the afternoon, though you could hardly measure the fact by the neutral gray of this bleak day. Bowie could gauge a day's length by his slow accumulation of saddle aches; a man acquired a built-in timepiece as he began to lose the green resilience of youth. The chill dampness reaching to his joints aggravated the usual twinges.

The six-man detail pushed their gather across the last rises and into the river valley. The big roundup bivouac sprawled across the lush-grassed bottoms. Six campfires were strung along the banks of the Oro, chuck wagons pulled up beside them. Both horsebackers and men on foot made moving shadows in the dull light. The freight and calf wagons were set off toward the big herd, which made a bawling, discordant mass south of the camp. The detail pressed their bunch into the herd, exchanged greetings with the guards, then turned their horses into the *remuda* tended by three wranglers.

Bowie and Sully separated from their companions, all men from another crew, and tramped tiredly toward their own wagon. Third from the north end of the line, it was drawn up in a motte of cottonwoods that slightly sheltered it from the weather. Gonzales, the Chainlink cook, was a gaunt Mexican so dourly cadaverous and hollow-eyed that an undertaker wouldn't believe it. He already had a big cow-camp coffeepot bubbling on a tripod over the fire, for the incoming riders were cold and wet tonight as well as tired. Bowie and Sully were among the first ones to arrive. They filled their tin cups and squatted by the fire, soaking up the heat.

Brady Trapp came tramping in with Joe-Bob and Trinidad. His green glance touched Bowie; his jaw hardened truculently against his beard. He rode a grudge like an Indian, Bowie thought. They'd seen plenty of each other these first two days of roundup, and each time they met, Bowie was aware of Brady's silent bridling.

"You pa, he is come to roundup a little while ago," said Gonzales.

"Yeah." Brady's tone was surly. "I seen him."

Presently Cyrus Trapp came up to the fire, resembling a bulky yellow grizzly in his slicker. His face seemed drawn and tired, as if he'd perceptibly aged in the few days since they'd seen him.

He spoke a greeting that included everyone.

"How's it going?" The question was directed to Sully.

"Fine," Sully said. "Everything's fine."

Which, Bowie knew, was Cyrus's quiet way of confirming that he'd been a good boy. That was all right. Man's privilege to learn how his gamble was paying off.

The mizzle was letting up. Dusk had started to thicken the gray murk. More men coming off work were drifting toward their fires, their forms blurry in the clotting dusk. Gonzales set a Dutch oven loaded with pans of freshly made bread in the fire and shoveled glowing coals on top of it. He hooked another Dutch oven out of the coals and knocked off the lid. The oven contained three inches of sizzling lard. Working swiftly, he cut many thin steaks the size of his palm from a beef quarter, rolled them in flour left over from his breadmaking, and dropped them into the hot fat. The savory smells began to melt the men's weary taciturnity. They guzzled steaming coffee and exchanged small talk.

Men continued to drift into camp. While they waited for supper, Brady Trapp cajoled three of them into a turn of cards. Bowie studied his avid face in the firelight as he dealt the pasteboards onto a dry square of canvas. Cyrus was drinking coffee and watching. Abruptly he dropped his empty cup in the wreck pan and walked off into the trees. It was presently clear why he couldn't abide watching. Brady became exultant as a kid each time the cards ran his way, then turned sullen and cursing when he lost each hand. It was an old story to the men looking on; they exchanged amused glances.

"He ever win a game?" Bowie asked dryly.

"Sure, when they let him. Call it politics." Sully shook his head. "Something to watch, ain't it? There's a man with a fever that won't burn out and no bottom to back it."

"Ain't half his pa's man, that's sure."

"He ain't. But he's strong as a bull and hard as rocks. Would bear that in mind if I was you."

"You trying to worry me?"

"I am telling you a fact you best stay on top of. Brady has got one mean burr up his ass where you're concerned. No mind what his pa told him, he ain't through with you."

"Hell, I know that."

Sully gave him a speculative, faintly baffled glance. Bowie walked out on the flats a few yards to stretch his legs. He halted, listening to the cattle and the camp noises, old and familiar sounds. Damned if it wasn't true, as old-timers always claimed, that the whole business got into a man's blood after a fair round of years. Gazing across the faintly lit flat where firelight carried, Bowie made out a spectral blot of white moving his way. A canvas-topped wagon, and it wasn't one that belonged to this roundup.

Someone came tramping up beside him. It was Faye Nevers, coffee cup in hand. Does he ever miss a damn thing? Bowie wondered.

"Looks like a Conestoga," Bowie said. "Emigrants?"

"Another damn sodbuster." Disgust thickened Nevers's voice. "Batting around in the dark miles from anywhere. One gets you ten he don't know where he is."

The wagon jolted toward them across the bunch grass, rolling and pitching. The driver pulled up abreast of them, his rough voice halting the team. He stared down at them, a stocky man with a pale ragged mustache and pale tufted brows above deep-set eyes. He was about forty. His broad face was sullenly pugnacious and there wasn't a jot of apology in his manner.

"What is this place?" He had a heavy accent that sounded German or Scandinavian.

"A roundup camp," Nevers said curtly. "You've come a way off your trail."

"Eh." The man squinted at a shimmer of water. "This is the Oro River?"

"That's right."

"Then I am not lost."

"Depends what the hell you're looking for."

"Bottomland. Good bottomland and water. I am told this is the best in the country."

"They tell you it's Chainlink range too?"

"They say it's public domain that is used by some cattle outfits. It can be filed for a homestead." The man's tone was surlily matter of fact. "This I am going to do."

Nevers was already shaking his head. "It's like

65

I told you. You're way off your trail, fella. Now you turn that ratty rig of yours around and get the hell off this land."

The man hunched forward, thick shoulders bunching against his frayed blanket coat. "You are the owner of this — Chainlink?"

"No. I am." Cyrus had joined them; he spoke calmly, flatly. "I'm Cyrus Trapp. What's your name?"

"It is Jan Ekstrom."

"You can file a claim anywhere up and down this river you're a mind to, Ekstrom. The law says so. See you leave my beef and horses alone while you're around. That won't be for long."

Cyrus was already turning away. Ekstrom said, "Wait!" He was scowling, his square blunt-fingered hands flexing around his reins. "You are saying you'll let me get started — then run me off?"

Cyrus moved his head in negation. "I won't need to lift a finger. You can't crop this country and make it pay. Growing season's way too short. You'll be wiped out in a year. Less."

"Why let him plow up good grass?" Nevers said angrily. "Man, I can —"

Cyrus raised a peremptory hand. From inside the wagon came a weak, fretful wailing, broken by little coughing noises. A baby. And a woman's soft voice soothing it in a foreign tongue: *"Sov nu, sov min pojke. . . ."*

"It's my wife and kid," Ekstrom said sullenly. He turned and spoke sharply into the open

66

canvas pucker at his back. Swedes, Bowie thought. He had spent one bitter-cold winter he'd as soon forget working in a Montana logging camp with Swedish and Norwegian lumberjacks. Ekstrom was telling her to quiet the kid.

But she gave back a spirited answer. Now the pale oval of her face showed in the pucker hole by her husband's shoulder. "Please — sir. My baby is sick." Her English was halting and broken. "Can you help us?"

Cyrus pulled off his hat. "I surely can, ma'am. Why didn't you say about the baby, Mister?"

"We ask for nothing," Ekstrom snapped.

"Doesn't matter what you ask or don't. Nobody in need ever got turned from my door. You'll lay over here tonight. We'll see what's to be done. Get your wagon under those trees. Faye, have someone take care of the team."

Ekstrom peered at him from under shaggy brows. Opened his mouth truculently, then closed it. Cyrus's manner was unmistakably that of a man accustomed to giving commands. A man ready to back up his word. Ekstrom put his team in motion and pulled up under the cottonwoods. After he had passed the baby down to Cyrus, Ekstrom gave his wife a hand down. Did it kind of roughly, Bowie thought.

Cyrus gently poked aside the blanket that hooded the baby's face. Laid a callused forefinger on the small forehead. "How old is he?"

"Eight months," the woman said. "Please, can

you do anything? All the time he coughs — for a week now."

"No wonder. Out in this weather, bumping along in a wagon. Running a fever too. Don't you people know better'n to go kiting off in the middle of nowhere with a sick infant?"

Mrs. Ekstrom nodded, fixing a level gaze on her husband as she spoke. "Already the baby was sick when we stop at Saltville. The doctor, he said what you say, Mister. Didn't he, Jan, eh?"

Ekstrom turned away, muttering to himself. It left little doubt where the responsibility lay. The crew looked on in curious silence as Cyrus handed the baby back to his mother, then tramped over to the chuck wagon.

"Mr. Gonzales, I want a piece of beef boiled up for broth. Nothing like it when a baby's ailing with croup." The cook nodded and dug a copper pot out of his wagon. Charlie the roustabout hauled the Dutch ovens from the fire; the crew got plates and lined up to receive their grub.

"Tomorrow I'll take you to my place," Bowie heard Cyrus tell the Ekstroms. "Only sensible thing to do. Baby wants proper caring for. I'll have Doc Rawls brought from Saltville."

Ekstrom glowered at him. "Why you do this for us? Eh?"

"Not for you." Cyrus's tone was dust-dry.

"It ain't your kid. Charity we don't need."

"Charity you don't get. You look husky enough to haul your own freight. Ever work cows?"

68

"Nah. Just the *milch* kind."

"You'll learn."

"*Helvete!* I did not come all the way from Minnesota —"

"Listen, Mister," Cyrus cut him off flatly. "This baby of yours is ailing bad. I know the signs. I lost a daughter to the croup when she was three years old. There's things we can do for your child at headquarters — keep him warm and dry, burn sulphur under a blanket tent. You tried that?"

"No," Mrs. Ekstrom murmured, rocking the feebly crying baby in her arms. "Oh, Jan. We must take this man's help, we must let him do what he can."

"Not much a man can do, but my womenfolk can lend a hand. Got a young Indian housekeeper knows medicine ways you wouldn't believe." Cyrus looked hard at Ekstrom. "Mister, you can go ahead and start your homestead like you want. You'll be lucky to get a cabin up before first snow. Meantime there'll be bitter frosts of a night and plenty of fall weather. Rain, sleet, weeks of it. And a bad-sick baby to worry about. You got any sense at all, you'll figure on wintering at Chainlink. You want some food, ma'am, I'll fetch you a plate."

"*Tack* — thank you."

Cyrus tramped over to the chuck wagon. Ekstrom walked stiffly away to the edge of firelight and stood with his back to the camp, hands rammed in his pockets, his shoulders hunched

69

with pride and anger and resentment. Cyrus fetched a crate for Mrs. Ekstrom to sit on, then brought her a plate of food and cup of coffee. He held the baby while she ate; he paced a slow circle, a bear-big man who cradled the tiny bundle as gently as a woman might.

"What's his name, Missus?"

"Eric."

"Fine name for a boy. You know, Missus, my girl 'ud be about your age if she'd lived. Could of been the proud grandpappy of a boy like Eric around now."

As the crew finished eating, they began clattering tin plates and cups into the wreck pan. Gonzales growled at them to keep the noise down; *Santa Maria,* with a sick *bebé* here, did they have no better sense? Cyrus handed the baby back to Mrs. Ekstrom, took her empty plate and cup to the wreck pan, then went over to the Dutch ovens to load a plate for himself. Gonzales had lifted the pot of broth from the fire; he carried it to his wagon tailgate and filled a cup with the steaming liquid.

"She's plent' hot, boss. I let her steep and cool before we give to *bebé*, eh?"

Cyrus grunted assent, leaning against a wagon wheel as he ate. Brady came tramping up to him and halted, feet apart. His stocky body was braced with a tense truculence. "Pa, I want to talk."

"All right. Talk."

"We better step off a ways."

Cyrus gave him a dour look, then laid his plate aside. The two walked around back of the wagon; Brady began talking in a low, heated voice. Bowie had been taking in the scene as he ate, overhearing most of what had been said. He dumped his utensils in the wreck pan and then, never a man to shy off from an impulse, walked over to Mrs. Ekstrom and her baby.

He touched his hatbrim. "Ma'am."

She raised her eyes with a small curious nod. Deep-lashed eyes that were finely gray, like night mist. She wasn't over twenty-five; her face was oddly tranquil in a resigned sort of way. She looked as if she might smile easily whenever she wasn't so worried and fine-worn.

Bowie peered at the baby's reddened face. Even between coughing spasms, it seemed to screw up as if from jabs of pain, the small body half-doubling. "Seems to me that is more'n the old croup, ma'am."

She nodded. "His little belly, it's very sore."

"Could be cramps from the coughing. Or maybe his innards got bruised some way. There's a tonic my ma used to make when one of us kids had a cold or a sore gut. Sort of a soothing syrup."

Gonzales came up with the cup of warm broth. "Now she's cool enough, you give him some of this, Señora."

"Oh, thank you. I do not know if he will take it. He does not take much to eat and maybe it will not stay down."

71

"Might be able to fix that with a dose of the old syrup," Bowie said. "Cook's got the makings in his wagon. I can fix some right away. Have to go into your kitchen, cook."

Gonzales nodded reluctantly. "Sure, if it help the little one. Here, Señora, hold the *bebé* so, and we give him some of this."

Bowie moved over to the wagon and set out the ingredients he needed. Tallow lard, black-jack sorghum, powdered alum from the medicine chest. He dropped some tallow in a cup and set it by the fire to melt. Poured another cup a third full of sorghum and, after a moment's hesitation, added a dash of alum. Stuff could fetch the baby some more belly pains if he had an open sore there, but it would also heal; just a dash would do. He'd added the melted fat to the sorghum and was waiting for the mixture to cool when an angry, heedless lift of voices carried from the motte of trees off behind the wagon. Cyrus and Brady had been talking quietly up till now.

". . . damn quick have every son-of-a-bitching rawhider in the country scrounging off us," Brady was saying bitterly. "Time was when we hustled trash like that off our open range straightway."

"All right," Cyrus rumbled with thinning patience. "We hustle him off. Then he goes to the federal marshal and we got real trouble. I told you times have changed. Biggest of us can't make the kind of tracks we used to in this country. There's law here now and it's come to stay."

"But Christ, Pa! Let one get away with it and you'll have a whole flood of his sort pouring in."

"No help for it. Law says that this man or anyone like him can file one hundred and sixty acres with the land office and make his improvements, and it's his. But none of 'em'll last. Nature'll see to it."

"What goddam difference will that make when they're done plowing it all to hell?" Brady said savagely. "You say you built up Chainlink for us, Joe-Bob and me. What'll there be left?"

"We got plenty patented land that's ours free and clear," Cyrus snapped. "Anyways it'll never go that far. The sodders'll give up before long. Now you simmer down."

"Goddammit, law's got nothing to do with way you started coddling rawhider trash! That damn drifter, this snorky and his family. Don't give me no more crap about old-time hospitality, you gone soft, that's the whole thing, plain goddam soft!"

"Not so soft I can't still bust you ass over tea-kettle." Cyrus's voice was notching upward with a quiet fury. "You — *uh!*"

"Pa — Christ, what is it? What's the matter?"

"Nothing that's concern of yours," Cyrus snarled. "Get the hell away —"

He came plodding out of the trees, head sunk between his shoulders like a ringy bull's. His face was ashen with pain; his eyes wore an unfocused glaze. He lurched across to his bedroll and collapsed on his back, throwing an arm over his eyes. An uneasy murmur ran through the crew. The incident had confirmed a possibility they'd begun to suspect and discuss in hushed mutters some time ago: that Cyrus, for all his giant's strength, was a desperately ill man.

Brady tramped into view now. His eyes, glassy with rage, fell on Bowie standing by the wagon only yards away. He came over to him, long arms swinging. "You get a good earful, bum?"

"Yeah."

"I ought to unscrew your goddam head right here!"

"I gave your pa my word. Maybe you didn't get it."

"I got it," Brady said hotly. "You handed him a string of taffy and he swallowed it. I don't!"

"I'll tell you, Junior. I'm tired of getting high-heeled by you. You want to settle things so damn bad, we can do it back of them trees."

Slowly and wickedly, Brady shook his head. "Not yet, bummer. There'll be a time. A place. I'll pick it. You wait."

CHAPTER FIVE

Sofie Ekstrom hummed contentedly as she sliced up onions and potatoes for the stew. Plenty of *sill och potatis* there must be, the way Jan liked it. How good to once more be able to dip into a root cellar for whatever she needed in the way of vegetables. It was like home again. Home in Sweden, or in Minnesota? Both, in a way. Coming to America at seventeen had meant tearing up one set of memories. But she had come to think of the Ekstrom farm in Douglas County, Minnesota, as home too, and there were so many Swedish settlers in the region that in most ways life had differed little from what it had been in *gamla hemlandet,* the old country.

Sofie had a need of roots and permanence. When Jan had announced his decision to sell the farm and move to a Western place, her reaction had been a panicked wish to hang on to all that was, the fixed comforts she'd come to know and be comfortable with. It was harder to tear up roots a second time; you were older, jelling in your ways, and making a change came harder.

Of course she should have supposed that something of the sort was brewing in Jan's head. The loss of his wheat crop two years in a row: first to drought, then to flattening hail. His restless mutterings of discontent. It couldn't be said that he'd ever shared his thoughts with her, being glum and close-mouthed at his best, surly and black-tempered at his worst, but rarely did his moods leave her in any doubt of his feelings. *Ja,* no doubt Jan's decision to leave Minnesota had been ripening for a long time and she merely hadn't wanted to believe it.

Eric let out an earsplitting yell and flailed his arms. Sofie went over to the long-unused crib that Mr. Trapp had dug out of the harness shed loft; she pulled up to Eric's chin the comforter that he'd kicked off. "We do not play now," she said. *"Var en snall pojke. Sov nu."* Eric wasn't interested in being a good boy or in going to sleep. He wanted attention and proclaimed it by giving a lusty good-natured squawl.

Sofie didn't mind in the least; she was smiling as she returned to cutting up vegetables. How fine it was to see him carry on like any normal baby. Eric had been rather sickly from birth; weeks in a jolting wagon, then the raw cold and wet, had slowly worsened his condition. In those last despairing days before Cyrus Trapp had taken them in, Sofie had felt a deepening dread for her child. And something else, as Jan Ekstrom had blindly, stubbornly refused to stop somewhere, anywhere, for the baby's sake. Something like the beginning of hatred for a man she had married out of an ill-defined sense of duty.

Yet Eric hadn't taken a real turn for the worst till just before they'd encountered the roundup outfit. By then, at last, Jan was feeling a flush of guilty alarm. She'd known this by how he had yielded, though with poor grace, to Cyrus Trapp's insistence on helping them.

Sofie glanced out one of the two small windows that fronted the single-room cabin. Dusk was a blue mist deepening toward purple, so the crew would be in soon. She quickly finished up the potatoes and dropped them in the stewpot. Jan would be home directly and be very ugly if he had to wait long on supper. *Home!* It was really coming to seem like that after only two weeks, and it surprised her that this should be, everything was so different from what she'd known. Yet not altogether, thanks to the kindness of these Chainlink people.

Mr. Trapp had insisted that the Ekstroms stay in the big house, where Eric might be properly looked after. A room had been prepared for them; everyone had outdone themselves fussing over the baby. Dr. Rawls was summoned from Saltville; Tula Calder had fixed many mysterious brews and poultices from plants she'd gathered. But Sofie wasn't sure that Eric's dramatic improvement wasn't due as much to the constant attentions of three women to his every need and comfort. Especially to the ministrations of childless Mrs. Trapp; her husband had confided to Sofie that Adah hadn't seemed so satisfied since he'd brought her to Chainlink. And what of Mr. Candler's wonderful syrup? For the first time in months, Eric's belly had ceased to hurt him. The remedy must have healed something in it, for after a few doses he had complained no more. The high thin air of this mountain valley and some nice fall weather of late had also helped, Dr. Rawls had told her. In any case, Eric's general health had not been so good since his birth.

Once the baby's improvement was certain, Cyrus Trapp had moved the Ekstroms to permanent quarters. This was the original cabin which he'd built on the headquarters site more than thirty years ago, the home to which he'd brought his first bride. It was furnished with such spare furniture, utensils, and so on as could be found, along with what the Ekstroms had brought in their wagon. A few repairs here and there, the logs freshly chinked and new shakes nailed on the roof, and it made as snug and weather-tight a home as one might wish.

From out by the corrals came the faint noises that indicated the crew was coming in. Sofie glanced out a window and made out the shadowy forms of men and horses. She hung the pot of stew on the fireplace lug and stoked up the fire, then began to set the table. Soon Jan came roughly through the door, yanking off his hat and coat. He stared grouchily at the table.

"Where's supper?"

"It will not be ready for awhile. Mrs. Trapp was here. She —"

"*Gud bevara,*" he growled, flinging his coat and hat on a wall peg. "That damn woman, she's got nothing to do but gad about all day, eh?"

"She is lonesome, Jan, and she likes the baby. She comes calling and I can't just tell her not to."

"She has got a housekeeper to do her work. That Injun *flicka*." He walked to the crib and stared bleakly down at the cooing Eric. Then went to a shelf, took down a bottle, and drew the cork with his teeth. "Let her talk to the Injun. You got work to do. Tell her that."

"Vaska dig," she said tartly. "Wash yourself before you start drinking."

Her day's contentment was already dampened. It was the same as always, as it had been through the four years of their marriage. She was glad of the long hard hours that kept him away from daybreak till dusk, here as back in Minnesota. But Jan hated this job of working beef cattle. "Maybe it will seem better in time," she had told him. "Now it's so new." But no; this work was hateful, it was beneath his pride, and he loathed working for anyone else. If not for Cyrus Trapp's generosity, she'd felt impelled to remind him, they'd have been in sorry straits; yet he hadn't voiced a word that might indicate gratitude. That, from Jan, was only to be expected.

What Sofie had not expected was that he'd take to whiskey to dull the edge of his resentment and frustration. Jan had never been much of a drinker except on holidays, and these occasions were really welcome; at such times he would be halfway pleasant, even boisterous sometimes. The kind of drinking he'd done of late, and he indulged every night, only emphasized the surly, taciturn ways that had grown on him year by year. Sometimes, too, he would yell and curse at her, which he'd never done before.

Grumbling, Jan washed up and toweled his head and hands, then got a cup and filled it from the bottle. Sofie noted, not for the first time, the avid tremble in his hand as it brought the cup to his mouth: she knew only too well what it meant. Drink was becoming the same disease in him that it had been in her father. She couldn't count the times in her girlhood that she'd put that luckless, foolish, gentle man to bed with his load of *schnapps* and self-pity. One problem, at least, that hadn't plagued her marriage. Till now.

Jan continued to drink, slumped in a chair. By the time she had supper on the table, he was blearily, morosely drunk as she couldn't remember seeing him. He stamped to the table and slid onto the bench, almost knocking it over. Sofie felt a stab of self-reproach: if she'd had the meal ready earlier, his nightly intake wouldn't have fallen on an empty stomach. He sluggishly spooned up the hot stew, spilling half of each mouthful. Sofie kept her eyes lowered and ate without appetite.

Someone rapped gently at the puncheon door. Almost with relief, she hurried to open it. Bowie Candler stood there; he touched his hat.

"Evening, ma'am. How is the boy?"

He had a swift laconic way of going to the point that disconcerted and amused her. "Oh —

he is fine now, *fint som snus*. Won't you come in, Mr. Candler?"

"No'm, thanks. Just dropped by to inquire after the boy. That sorghum-tallow mix still settling his belly all right?"

"Oh, yes. But I have not had to give it to him lately. His belly is all well now."

"That's good." Candler touched his hat again. "Night, ma'am."

He turned and was gone. Thoughtfully Sofie closed the door.

What a strange man! She had mentioned his kindness to Mrs. Trapp, who had given a slight shudder and called Candler a tough, a tramp, below a decent person's notice, and said she couldn't understand why Cyrus had hired him. To Sofie he'd merely seemed abrupt, not a man to waste words. One who showed his streak of kindness in perfunctory flashes, as if he shunned the notion of anyone getting too close to him. Yes, a strange man . . .

As she came back to the table, Jan said heavily: "What's that fellow want?"

"Didn't you hear?" She sat down and picked up her spoon. "He asked about the baby. Eric's belly is all better for that syrup he show me how to make."

"How often does he come around?"

She looked up, startled by the open hostility in his face. "Why, he has called twice in two weeks. He only ask about the baby. *Himmel,* what is wrong —"

"I don't want that fellow around here!" His fist banged on the table. "You hear me? Tell him to stay away!"

"You are a *dumskalle!*" She bit her lip in anger. "I tell him nothing. You tell him what you want."

"Maybe you like bums coming around, eh?" His voice slurred drunkenly; he changed to Swedish, spitting out the words. "I will not tolerate a *gris* like that around my wife. Even if she has taken a fancy to pigs."

Sofie got to her feet, feeling the choke of all her stored-up fury and disgust. "You are the pig. Not only a pig but the biggest fool God has made. I will not talk to you."

"No, you will not talk *that way* to me —"

He was on his feet, clumping unsteadily around the table toward her. Beyond his raised hand she saw the mad glitter of his eyes. He hit her hard, flat-handed. The blow swiveled her head; tears jetted from her eyes.

"Clear the table. Then ready yourself for bed. It's time you remembered who your husband is."

He stamped back to the bench, gave his plate a bearlike swipe that sent it clattering to the floor, and went to his chair and collapsed into it. He picked up the bottle. Sofie stood with her head down, hand pressed to her cheek. He could have hit her much harder. But he'd never hit her at all before. Numbly she began to gather the dishes from the table and carry them to the battered wreck pan.

Afterward she went to the crib and gazed down at the sleeping Eric. She felt suddenly forsaken and alone, as she hadn't felt since her father had died. *Min lille gosse.* My little boy. He is all there is.

Jan cleared his throat: it held a warning note.

She went over to the bed that was built into one corner of the room, undressed slowly, and lay down. He came across the room, fumbling along the table for support. He said something hoarse and inarticulate; it ended in a labored belch. As he loomed above her, she turned her mind to a stony nothing. To a blank unfeeling wall. Then shut her eyes as his weight came down on her.

CHAPTER SIX

Brady Trapp threw down his hand of cards with a curse, scraped back his chair, and stood up. He glared at the three crewmen still seated at the table in the smoky, ill-lighted bunkroom. "Deal me out. Had enough of you bastards and your bellystripping for one night."

"You get any more small change burning through your pocket, drop around," one of them drawled. The others laughed.

Brady wished that one of them had taken offense. He was in the mood to hit somebody. But none took offense; they never did. They enjoyed pampering his gaming fever, cracking jokes at his expense, taking the few coins he could dredge up for these penny-ante turns of poker. Momentarily he toyed with a notion of provoking one or a couple of them, he wasn't particular, to a free-for-all. But Faye Nevers's chill stare damped the idea. The foreman lay in his bunk, dragging on a cigarette as he watched. Damn Faye; a man never knew what he was thinking.

Swinging toward the door, Brady halted as it was pushed open and Bowie Candler came in. He had stepped out a while ago. Brady stood flat-footed in Candler's path, not budging. But Candler only crossed his livid stare with an indifferent one, skirted around him, and went to his bunk. Brady tramped out, slamming the door, and headed for the big house. Each time he saw that goddam drifter, the urge to bust his jaw ate deeper.

He shivered at the deepening hint of fall in the chilly night; a familiar worry prodded his mind. Maybe the best solution, he thought glumly, was to throw himself on the old man's mercy. Lucky Jack Hackett in Saltville was getting impatient for his money. Brady's new run of IOUs with him ran over a thousand dollars. If he didn't cough up soon, Hackett would drop the fat in the fire himself by going directly to Cyrus.

Brady dreaded the thought. Better if Cyrus got it straight from him. Not much better, though. Cyrus had coupled his paying off of Brady's debts two years ago with a hard promise. If Brady didn't straighten up and stay straightened, he'd burn his old will and have new instructions drawn up: Chainlink to be sold at public auction after his death and the money split among a half-dozen shirttail relatives. A limited sum to be set aside for Joe-Bob; for Brady, nothing. It was no bluff; Cyrus didn't bluff.

Christ, Christ! There had to be some way out of this goddam pickle. Some way . . .

He tramped onto the back porch and into the kitchen. Tula was washing dishes in the big copper sink; for once Brady forgot to ogle her lustfully. He went to the cookie jar, dipped out a fistful of cookies, seated himself at the kitchen table, and scowled at the floor.

Two voices were raised in the parlor.

Sounded like Cyrus was het up about something and Adah was trying to placate him. He'd been getting proddy as hell lately as those head pains had worsened. Old fool hadn't the sense to see a doctor; too damn proud even to admit anything was wrong. Well, that was his lookout. Just that it was a damn nuisance being wakened every couple nights by his damn groaning.

Brady considered the implications with a sudden calculation. Just how serious *was* whatever the hell was ailing him?

Then he thought bleakly: forget it. Couldn't count on anything for sure regarding Cyrus's illness. One thing certain was that Lucky Jack could pull the roof down on him, Brady, any time. He crammed another cookie in his mouth, all his bitter frustration swelling back now. Again he considered making a clean breast to the old man. Decided once and for all against it. But there had to be *something — !*

Brady's moving jaws stopped. Maybe. He thought of Red Antrim and his crowd of tough nuts. They were a shiftless gang of ne'er-do-wells who spent most of their time hanging around Hackett's and other Saltville dives, gambling, drinking, picking quarrels. They always had a few dollars to carouse with, and rumor had it they engaged in whiskey-selling to the Utes and a few other shady sidelines. Complaints had been lodged from time to time, but nothing was ever found to firmly implicate

Antrim's blue-ribbon outfit.

Yet — Brady puckered his brow, remembering how Antrim had bought him a drink last time he'd been in town and then let fall a sly suggestion. Brady, having dropped another bundle at the tables that night, had been in a particularly vile mood. Proceeding to get monumentally drunk, he'd been swimming in a boozy fog when Antrim had made his proposal. Matter of fact, he'd flared up and almost swung on Antrim. Now, trying to recall what Antrim had said, he could only summon up a few dim and disjointed bits. But that little was enough to warm him with a slow excitement.

Brady pondered it carefully. The idea carried a high risk. But it could be the way out if Antrim had meant what he'd said. And he'd be a damn fool to broach such a suggestion if he hadn't.

Adah came briskly into the kitchen, her face paler than usual. "Tula, is there any coffee left from supper?"

"Yes, ma'am. I'll heat it."

"If it's still warm, that won't be necessary."

Adah crossed to the cupboard and took down a tin cup; she went to the stove and felt the coffeepot. Brady watched her with a mild curiosity. His youthful stepmother was easy to look at, but she was too proper and lah-de-dah to stir up in him what Tula, bronze-skinned and free-moving, could. Or that Ekstrom's wife. Man, there was a lush piece. Damned shame she had to be wasted on a miserable hoegrubber.

87

"You change your brand?" Brady asked idly. "Thought tea was your poison."

Adah filled the cup and turned from the stove; worry glided shadowlike behind her eyes. "It's for your father. I think you should know — he has been drinking."

"Yeah?" Brady began to grin. "You whip him up a jigger of lemonade, Miz Adah?"

"It's no laughing matter. He is drinking whiskey."

Brady stared at her. He swung the chair, clapping his hands on his knees. "You serious?" He saw that she was. "Why, holy hell, he's never taken a drink in his life!"

"You mean in *your* life."

"Never that I seen him, I mean." Brady chuckled. "Never been bluenosed about it; we always had booze around for anyone fancies it. Hell, I never really thought about it."

"You'd better think about it now. Mr. Nevers told me that Cyrus can't take strong drink — not as other men can."

"What's that mean?"

"I think I am finding out." The cup was trembling in Adah's hand; she clasped both hands tight around it. "One of his headaches began a while ago — the pains were particularly severe. He took a drink — then another — to blunt them. It seemed to work. But his whole manner changed — almost violently. His language became — coarse and abusive. And now he is drinking more. Excuse me."

She brushed out of the kitchen. Frowning with curiosity, Brady rose and slowly followed her to the parlor. As he entered, Adah was saying: "Please, Cyrus, take the coffee. It will —"

Cyrus was standing by the walnut sideboard, leaning one spread hand on it. The other hand was fisted around a half-filled tumbler. An open bottle of J. H. Cutter stood at his elbow. His head was bent and now he slowly raised it and heeled around. Brady felt a thin shock. Cyrus's face had a red thickened look; his mouth was half open.

"Cyrus?" Adah said anxiously. "Please —"

His arm swept up and knocked the cup from her hands, spraying coffee across the carpet. Adah gave a small cry and retreated from him. Cyrus stood with legs planted apart, squeezing the tumbler in his fist. He stared at Brady, wagging his head blindly; his words came slow and labored.

"Don't — you sons a bitches — tell me what t' do."

Brady licked his lips, "Listen — Pa. You better slack off before, uh, before you hurt yourself."

"Slack off — y'self — you bastard. Smash y' goddam teeth — clean down y' throat."

Jesus, Brady thought, he don't know me. What the hell? He advanced slowly toward Cyrus, putting out his hand. "You just ease off, Pa. Hand me that glass."

Cyrus swayed on his feet, hands clenching; his eyes glistened with a bloodshot fury. The tumbler cracked in his fist. He squinted and

89

growled, opening his hand; bloody glass shards tinkled on the carpet.

Adah screamed.

Cyrus was already moving in on Brady; his red-dripping hand rose. Brady stumbled wildly away, but his father's powerful backswing caught him flush on the jaw. The blow spun Brady half around; as he fought to catch his balance, both of Cyrus's hands clamped on his neck.

"Paaa —"

The word choked off in his throat. Cyrus's great weight carried him backward and hammered him against the wall. Brady tugged at his father's wrists, but he was half stunned as it was, everything blurring away in his sight. The hands squeezed and tightened. His eyes popped; his tongue swelled from his mouth. His last sensibility faded on the sound of Adah screaming again and again. . . .

Adah had never felt such unnerving terror. In these first stunned moments as Cyrus began strangling his son, she could only stand numbly, unbelievingly, and scream. And then Tula came running into the room, a skillet in her hands.

The half-breed girl didn't hesitate. A quick turn and she was behind Cyrus, rising the heavy skillet two-handed and crashing it down on his hunched back. He let go of Brady and swung around with a roar. Tula darted nimbly away, half-circling from him, holding the skillet ready. Cyrus lurched after her, crazy-eyed.

Adah didn't wait to see what happened next. She threw open the front door and ran across the porch. Fell going down the steps, landing on her hands and knees. She scrambled up and, heedless of shattered dignity for once, started running again, clenching her skirts, panicked sobs tearing in her throat. Cyrus . . . God, oh God, what had happened with him? What —

One blind thought filled her mind: to reach the bunkhouse and Faye Nevers. But she'd only covered half the distance when a man loomed out of the dark yard ahead. A startled cry escaped her. And she saw it was Nevers, coming on the run.

He caught her by the arms. "What is it? What's all the — ?"

"It's Cyrus — he's crazy, oh, God, he's drinking and he's crazy —"

Already he was brushing past her, heading for the house in great loping strides. He plunged across the porch and through the door. Adah, still holding her muddied skirts, started after him. As she came onto the porch, there was a crash of falling furniture and breaking glass.

Adah stopped in the doorway. Cyrus must have lunged at the retreating Tula, for she stood just beyond him and Cyrus lay sprawled on the upended taboret he'd fallen across, a scatter of broken gimcracks littering the floor. He was heaving laboriously to his feet as Nevers advanced slowly into the room, his voice gentle and placating.

"Easy, Cyrus. Just ease off there —"

Cyrus reared upright, shook himself like a ruffled bear, and glared around. There was no recognition in his eyes; they still wore an unheeding sheen of madness. He growled at Nevers; he started toward him, arms lifting. "Don't!" Adah heard herself cry. But the cry wasn't directed at Cyrus; it was for Nevers, warning him not to get in range of Cyrus's great crushing arms. She knew his great crushing strength too well, the strength she'd felt and silently feared even at his gentlest times.

Nevers, though, didn't try to close with him. He moved back and around, easy as a big cat, retreating while he kept quietly talking to Cyrus. He came to a stop by the sofa, and then Cyrus bulled straight for him. Nevers's arm dipped and snatched up an Indian blanket on the sofa; he stepped sideways and whipped the blanket at Cyrus's face as he charged past. It wrapped around Cyrus's head; he jerked to a bellowing halt and grabbed at its muffling folds.

Nevers took one long step, yanking out the pistol rammed in his belt. His arm lashed up and down; the gun-barrel thunked like an ax as it slammed Cyrus at the thick-muscled joining of neck and shoulder. His knees folded; he toppled. His fall shook the room, his forehead banging hard on the floor.

"Oh God," Adah said in an agonized whisper.

Brady was sprawled on his side by the wall, making feeble wheezing sounds. Nevers gave him an impersonal glance. "What happened to the son and heir?"

"Mr. Trapp was choking him," Tula said calmly. "I had to hit Mr. Trapp to stop him."

"That's too bad."

Nevers sounded ambiguous, almost indifferent. He knelt by Cyrus and eased him over on his back. He was out cold, his body heavy and loose. A redness of mashed skin stained his forehead. Nevers raised his head and stuffed a soft pillow under it. He felt of Cyrus's neck and shoulder where he'd struck him and then looked up at the women.

"Hit him pretty hard, but it had to be done. Fetch some cold water and cloths. We'll bring him around and get him to his room."

Tula went out to the kitchen. Her brother Sully appeared at the front door, two other crewmen crowding behind him. "What's happened?"

"It's over," Nevers said. "I had to put Cyrus out. Been drinking. We can handle him all right."

Sully gave a slow nod, as if he knew about Cyrus's problem. He turned to the others. "Let's clear out, boys." They tramped out the door, Sully closing it behind them.

Adah dropped on her knees by Cyrus's head, kneading her underlip between her teeth. It was an effort to hold her voice steady. "Will he be all right?"

"Nothing busted." Nevers gave her a quiet,

speculative look. "You all right?"

Her answer was a tight bitter nod. "Oh, yes."

Tula returned with a pot of water and some clean dishtowels. Nevers wet one and laid it on Cyrus's forehead. Brady was sitting up now, his back against the wall. His eyes were still glazed with shock and pain, his neck mottled with darkening bruises; all he could get out were tortured huskings of sound. Tula handed him a wet towel and he shakily held it to his bruised throat.

"Crazy . . . old . . . bastard," he finally managed to whisper. "Near . . . killed me. You better . . . tie . . . him up."

Nevers gave him a pointed look. "You better tie up your jaw. After you thank the girl. Seems she saved your — hide."

Tula glanced up from bandaging Cyrus's cut hand. "I did nothing for him," she said calmly. "I did it for Mr. Trapp."

"You — !"

Brady's voice failed him. He climbed unsteadily to his feet and stumbled out of the room. His footsteps slogged up the stairs. The bind of fear was unloosening in Adah's throat; her gaze briefly crossed Nevers's and then fell away. His intense yet expressionless eyes made her uneasy.

Cyrus moaned faintly; his bearded lips fluttered open. He began to stir. "Let's get him upstairs," Nevers said. "Girl, lend me a hand. Mrs. Trapp, you go on up and light a lamp."

Adah's legs felt shaky as she ascended the staircase. Coming onto the landing, she could

94

hear Brady's soft groans from his room. Joe-Bob's door swung open; he stood shirtless in the lamplight, blinking and buttoning his trousers over his underwear. He ran a hand through his tousled hair, yawned, and gaped at her.

"Hey, what's goin' on?"

Unbelievable, Adah thought. Sleeping was Joe-Bob's foremost pastime and he had slumbered through most of the commotion downstairs. "Nothing," she said. "Go back to bed." She entered Cyrus's room and felt for the matches and lamp on the commode. As a sickly glow of light spread across the room and its almost ascetic furnishings, she felt a hard knot of revulsion form in her throat. *He* slept here. Except for those times, mercifully rare of late, when he visited her room. This one reflected its tenant: rough, direct, uncompromising in his strength.

Adah threw back the bedcovers on the narrow bed; Nevers and Tula came in, supporting Cyrus's drag-footed hulk. He was muttering incoherently, his eyes strange and opaque. They laid him on the cot; Nevers wrestled off his boots. Joe-Bob came to the doorway and peered anxiously at his father, but didn't say anything.

"Best leave him as is," Nevers said. "Can't be sure how he'll be as he comes around, but my guess is he'll just sleep it off." He glanced at Adah. "You want, I can send a couple men to sit guard."

"That won't be necessary. He should be all

right now." The calmness of her own voice surprised her. "And Brady and Joe-Bob are nearby."

She pulled the covers over Cyrus and turned down the lamp. Joe-Bob had entered his brother's room; Adah heard his hushed question, Brady's whispery snarled reply, as she and Nevers and Tula descended to the parlor. Tula righted the overturned taboret and began picking up the bits of broken china. Adah felt like crying. Her treasured figurines, all in fragments. Maybe she would cry later.

As Tula exited from the parlor, Adah met Nevers's searching look. "I don't know," she murmured. "I just don't know."

"Get him to see a doctor."

"But he won't. I told you."

"Try again. You can see how out of hand the situation's got." He nodded at the liquor sideboard. "Get rid of all the hooch. Throw it out. That for a start. Then talk to him."

"I'll — try."

"You're the only one has a beggar's chance of making him listen." He moved closer, towering in front of her. "I know Cyrus. Whatever you say to him, even if he gets mad, no need to fear he'll be like that again. Not without booze in him."

"I know. That doesn't worry me. It's just — Can you guess how it's been? Half the night, every night, listening to him toss and moan? I don't think I can stand very much more."

"You know what I think? You're tougher than you know."

A smile turned up his lip corners; small lights kindled in his eyes. As if for this moment he'd let his careful guards slip to show her more than he ever had. But I knew all along, she thought, feeling the overpowering thrust of his masculinity as she had before. She felt her face go warm. Heat tendriled in her veins; her breasts tingled. If he hadn't glimpsed behind her prim composure as yet, God, how could he fail to now?

"You needn't worry. I will be all right."

He half-raised a hand. Didn't quite touch her arm. Turned wordlessly and went out the door, closing it gently behind him. Adah stood rubbing her wrists. A light shiver ran through her. Then she straightened, her mouth firming, and went upstairs again. As she entered Cyrus's room, he raised his head. His eyes were sick and groggy, but rational now.

"My good God." His lips hardly moved. "What — what happened down there?"

"It's all right now, dear. You had too much to drink."

Cyrus groaned. "Any at all's too much. My God." His hand reached and caught hold of hers. "Honey, I can't take a drink, never could, I —"

"Mr. Nevers has explained that."

"If I'd hurt you. If I'd hurt anybody . . ."

"Nobody's hurt. Dear, will you listen to me

now? I want you to see a doctor. I can't take any more of what's been. Do you understand?"

He was silent a long while, staring at the beamed ceiling. Finally: "Know where I was first two days of roundup? Why I didn't go out with the crew?"

"You went to Saltville. On business, you said."

"Business. I seen Doc Rawls. Stayed over a night so's he could make all the tests he wanted."

"And what — ?"

"Wasn't sure of anything. Said I'd need to see a specialist in Denver. I been putting it off."

"Then Cyrus, please . . ." Her voice turned softly vehement. "Don't put it off any longer! Not one more day."

"Don't mean to. I'll ride to Saltville to-morrow. Take the train from there."

Watching him, she felt an unexpected surge of affection. Not for the man she had tried to love and couldn't. For the guardian and benefactor whose kindly fortitude had borne her up through her father's final illness and afterward. What she felt for Cyrus Trapp the man was pity: the awful pity of a giant in pride and strength being steadily reduced to a helpless pain-wracked ruin.

"Cyrus — didn't he have *any* idea?"

"Doc? He just couldn't be sure."

It sounded evasive, Adah thought.

"Will find out in Denver what's what." Cyrus's lips twitched; his face looked grayish and old. "Doc wanted to give me laudanum for

98

when the pains come. Wouldn't take it. But I will do whatever the Denver man so says. You got my word to that."

CHAPTER SEVEN

"They been pushing 'em through right here," said Sully. "Through Yellow Pass and back into the Breaks. We found some heavy sign there and nowhere else."

Standing by the big map of Chainlink range that was tacked to the wall above Cyrus's desk, he traced a finger across the northwest corner. Cyrus leaned forward and peered through his glasses, then eased back in his chair. "Well, that would figure right. There are damn few places you could run beef through the Elks if you want to make a northerly market. Then it would have to be fifty miles to Craigie or over east to Sundog."

Sully nodded. "You drove your herds up to Craigie years ago, didn't you?"

"Sure, before the railroad run a spur line over to Saltville. All the big outfits hereabouts did. But we swung way west around the Elks. Long drive to a railhead, but you couldn't push a sizable herd straight across all that mean country in the Breaks. Bust your cows' legs all to hell, run a hundred pounds off each one. But move 'em in small bunches like these jacklegs been doing, and if a man ain't in no hurry, no reason it couldn't be done."

"So now we start hunting the Breaks?" Sully asked.

Cyrus grunted. "You don't know that country like I do, boy. Take us months to comb it all. Once they're through Yellow Pass, the thieves can scatter their sign to hell and gone. Must be holding the cattle in one place, but they could reach it by a dozen different ways. There's rock stretches they can drive across and cover their trail easy, long as they only take a few head at a time."

Heaving out of his chair, he paced slowly around his office, rolling a well-chewed cigar between his jaws. Sully gave Bowie, who was slacked in a chair by the door, a wry glance. Both men were dirty, unshaven, dog-tired. For three days they'd been scouring the wild and rugged country along Chainlink's north range in an effort to turn up something certain about the thieves' operation.

Chainlink line riders had begun to notice signs of strange horsemen a couple of weeks back, sign that was scattered but a lot of it. They had been pushing cattle. A ranch this size, whose north boundary lay along the Elk Breaks, a shallow, barren, broken terrain that slashed deep between mountains, was bound to be plagued with penny-ante thieving by backhill ne'er-do-wells. This was different. Only the next range tally would show the loss with any accuracy, but the sign which kept cropping up indicated steady strikes. No large single ones, just quick drive-offs of small bunches, furtively and by night, but they were adding up.

Cyrus paced heavily, scowling at the floor. "Gentlemen, somebody has put some thought behind this. They are hitting at irregular times and at wide-apart spots. Cutting chances of getting caught by breaking up the pattern. That is clear, but other things ain't."

"Like how they mean to peddle the stuff," Bowie said idly.

"Yeh. We got bummers hereabouts who'll steal a cow or so for the beef or for hides and tallow. But these bastards got to be stealing for profit. Suppose they vent the brands and try to sell the beeves at Sundog or Craigie. Even if the buyer himself is crooked as a dog's hind leg, he knows the yards'll demand a bill of sale from the original owner. They don't get it, they will hold the beeves, wire the owner, and credit him for the cattle."

"Ain't like you to wait till that happens," Sully observed dryly.

"Ain't likely it will, either," Cyrus said impatiently. "These people know the Breaks country, which argues they are local. Maybe a clutch of them spindly-shanked hill trash who've thrown in together. Maybe some hardcase crew like Red Antrim's. Whoever, they got to know they can't peddle vented Chainlink stock in this part of the territory and not get caught. Argues they got something up their sleeves I can't rightly tell as yet."

Sully dropped into Cyrus's swivel chair, extended his legs, and crossed his boots. "Fine. So you tell the sheriff. But Sam Beamis can't do more'n we can."

"That's right. He'd have to pay a couple deputies to do the same and no telling how long it'll take."

"What you got in mind?"

"Catching 'em in the act," Cyrus said flatly. "We don't know where they'll hit next or where they been taking the cattle. But they been moving 'em through Yellow Pass till now. All right, when they try it again, we'll have a couple men up by the pass."

Sully raised his brows. "They could be up there a long time."

Cyrus nodded, rubbing a hand along his temple. It was a thoughtful gesture, not an anguished one. Sometimes, like now, his eyes were clear, his mind as keen as ever. Other times he seemed stuporous and dull, moving like a man drunk or drugged. The crew had done a lot of quiet speculating about it. Everyone was sure that Cyrus's abrupt trip to Denver had been for other than business reasons. Those times he was heavy-eyed and slow-moving, they figured, he was full of drugs he'd been given for the head pains. But nobody was sure what his real trouble was.

"It's no job for daisies," Cyrus went on. "The men'll have to watch day and night, spelling each other. They'll have to stay out of sight. No fire. They'll have to keep a cold camp, and there's been an ice scum on the water bucket

103

every morning for a week now. They want to cook their grub, one'll have to move a mile or so away from the pass and lay a fire. Smoke seen hard by the pass could undo everything. One man's got to stay on guard all times. Hell, you wouldn't want the job."

Sully made a wry face. "Sounds like a bitch of a stand."

"It will be. That's why I'm asking, not ordering. I want these people trailed if they show up. Want to find where they're holding the cattle. I want the men too. But we can take 'em later if we know where they are. All the same, you could run into gunplay."

Sully nodded, modestly studying the toe of his boot. "Can't be no question who's the best tracker on your crew. And a mean shot to boot. Seems I'm volunteering."

"I figured you was too big-headed not to." Cyrus swiveled a glance at Bowie. "What about you?"

"What about me?"

Cyrus snorted softly. "Forget it, Candler. You don't want to go on a stand like this one. Man could get his toes frostbit. Even catch a bullet. Like I said, it's no job for a daisy."

Bowie felt a stirring of anger. The old bastard. He knew exactly how to lay it to each man who worked for him. How to touch a man's pride, if he had any. "I'll take it, and the hell with you."

"Good," Cyrus said blandly. "You boys get a

104

night's sleep and head for the pass first thing to-morrow. Take enough grub for two weeks. I'll tell Gonzales to have it packed and ready in the morning." He paused. "One thing more. We'll keep what's been said here between us three. Anyone asks, I'm sending you up to our east line shack. That's a goodly ways from the Pass."

Leaving the office by an outside door at the house's southwest corner, Bowie and Sully headed for the bunkhouse. It was late in the day; a curdled-looking sunset was souring in the west and a hard wind was blowing off the peaks. Bowie shivered and rammed his hands deep in the pockets of his mackinaw, thinking bleakly of the October days and nights that lay ahead. An open fireless camp in the high country. Rain, freezing sleet, maybe snow, before the job was over. Or maybe he'd get lucky and catch a bullet. Christ!

"Damned old fart," he muttered. "Knows right where to grab a man when he's got a mean job wants doing."

"Well," Sully grinned, "you're learning."

"What I should of learned first of all was keep my goddam mouth shut. I dropped mention I'd trailed and hunted horses for a living, so I get sent out with you to round up sign on them rustlers. Shitkicker and me ain't warmed our heels in three days, now this."

Sully laughed and shook his head. "Leave it to you to give the buckskin a name like Shitkicker."

"Why not? Damn good name for a horse."

105

They cut past the weathered log house that the Ekstroms were occupying. Sofie Ekstrom was in the yard removing her day's wash from the clothesline, her skirt furling in the wind below a bulky coat. She waved and called, "Hello, Mr. Candler," the wind almost snatching her words away.

Bowie nodded and tugged his hatbrim. "How's the baby?"

"What? What did you say?"

"I said, *how's the baby?*"

"Oh, oh. *The baby is fine — fint som snus!*"

Bowie's mouth stretched in a grin he couldn't stop. "That's fine."

"What?"

"I said that's fine. *Fine as snuff!*"

"Oh, *ja!*"

Her bright laughter spilled out. And quickly stopped; she turned back to her task as the cabin door opened. Ekstrom stood in the doorway, legs braced wide. His face was red and angry; he yelled something at her in Swedish.

"That son of a bitch got born with a sour belly," Sully observed as they tramped on. "You notice that big bruise on her jaw?"

Bowie nodded and didn't say anything.

Yellow Pass was a funnel-shaped wedge in the deep foothills below the first peaks, broad at its mouth and tapering back to a narrow cleft hardly wide enough to drive single cows through. But it gave access to all sorts of possible trails in the wild Breaks beyond. Bowie and Sully bivouacked high on a timbered bluff to one side of the wide canyon mouth. Their camp was in a sheltered pocket back in the trees, but they kept a vigil from a granite shelf that gave a clean view of the pass and the rolling country that faced it, the edge of Chainlink's north range.

The days passed slowly. It was a damned boring stand to be stuck on, but at least they were favored by fairish weather. The early fall rains had passed; the wooded ridges were a vista of molten color, scarlets and russets and golds. The dawns were nippy with frost that yielded reluctantly to the pale sunlight of later morning. Afternoons were tolerably warm or cool, but soon gave way to the swift chilly twilights. Much of the time Bowie shivered on watch, hunkered on the shelf wrapped in three blankets, and he shivered off to restless sleep between watches. Could of been down in the border country by now, ran his frequent thought. God damn!

Still, it wasn't all cold and boredom. Only one man was needed on watch; the other could use his off hours to prowl for game, so long as he did it away from the pass. Cyrus had cautioned them not to fire a gun close by it. And Sully was a pretty good man to be stuck up here with, Bowie admitted to himself. They worked well as a team, a fact that he guessed Cyrus Trapp had given due consideration.

After five days, the thieves still hadn't tipped their hand.

"Don't see why in hell they don't make a move," Bowie grumbled. "They drove off some beeves in the pass not two days before we found the sign. And plenty of tracks that was made before then. They was using this way regular. Goddammit, I wonder if we got taken notice of some way."

"Not likely," said Sully. "No way them shorthorns could spot us before we see them. We ain't fired a shot or made a smoke inside a mile since we took up the stand. No way it could leak out neither, with just Cyrus knowing about us. Likely these jaspers are just playing it cagey. They was hitting fast and hard for maybe a couple weeks. Now they slacked off for a time."

"Maybe they got so cagey they quit. We're likely freezing our asses off up here for nothing."

"Ain't for nothing. Paleface soft. Teachem to count his blessings."

"Go to hell."

Sully shook his head sadly. "Sometimes I think paleface not appreciate good company."

"I do. That's the trouble."

They were squatting side by side on the shelf in the gray light of a late afternoon. Wet needles of sleet slapped against their clothing and stung their bent faces. Might have known the last week's weather had been too good to last, Bowie thought disgustedly.

"You don't fool me, white brother. I know that under your stony hide there beats a heart of solid flint." Sully yawned and peered at the sky.

It was roiling with great lead-colored clouds driving ominously out of the north. "Hell might not be a bad place to winter, at that. Devil keeps a warm hearth. And from the look, I'd say we are going to get a whole lot of weather dumped on us before nightfall."

Sofie Ekstrom kept fighting sleep. Her eyes were heavy and redly throbbing. No matter how hard she tried to stay alert and stiffly upright on the hard straight-backed chair, her mind would start drifting in a saffron fog, her body would cant sideways. Then she would catch herself. God, don't let me sleep. Don't . . .

Aware of the door softly opening behind her, she lifted her head. Adah Trapp had entered the room. Tiptoeing over to the bed, she gazed down at Eric. Touched his forehead, which Sofie knew was dry and hot. Adah looked searchingly at her now.

"Mrs. Ekstrom."

"Uh?"

"Please — why don't you lie down a while? You haven't had a wink of sleep in two days and nights."

"No — I do not sleep."

Adah frowned with a kind of vexed compassion. "At least let me bring in a comfortable chair for you."

"No," Sofie said dully. "Then I go to sleep for sure. I must be ready if he need me."

From the first it had seemed very important

109

that she stay awake. Eric might need her any moment, yet there was really nothing she could do. Nothing. Only a dim and dogged reflex held her stubbornly by her baby's side, listening to his weak, faint fits of coughing and the even more ominous silences between.

Adah said gently, insistently, "But you can't well tend him, don't you see, when you're so terribly exhausted. A few hours' sleep would do wonders for you. Tula and I can keep watch as well as you, and let you know at once if anything happens."

Adah had made the argument before. Sofie couldn't remember how many times before and didn't care. She moved her head in negation. "No. I must be here then."

"That is foolish," Adah said sharply. "Look at you, all but falling off that chair. Could you stay on if you weren't holding on?"

Sofie's hands were clenched on either side of her chair seat. She raised one hand and looked at it dull-eyed. It was swollen at the knuckles, welted red across the palm from the hard-cornered wood. She felt her body sway heavily and grabbed at the chair edge again.

"I guess I would fall." The matter-of-fact words made a trailing hum in her ears.

If only she had not left Eric alone. That single guilty refrain kept stabbing through her dead exhaustion. But the baby had seemed well, so well and healthy these three weeks past, that she'd failed to realize he couldn't throw off his frail sickliness since birth so quickly. But *himmel,* he had been on his way to getting better. And then suddenly, so suddenly, it was all undone.

Only two days and nights? The nightmare of waiting seemed endless. It had begun so thoughtlessly, so easily, her leaving Eric alone for the very first time. Mr. Trapp had given the crew a day off and all had gone to town except for Jan. But she and Jan had quarreled about something, *ja,* the drinking it was, and he had cuffed her several times and then, since there was no more liquor in the house, had followed the others to town. Though glad enough to have him gone, she'd become restless and worried as the day wore toward evening. She'd decided to visit the big house for a brief chat with Mrs. Trapp. For once she hadn't taken Eric along; as he was sound asleep, she would not disturb him, and she'd be back in a few minutes.

The storm had been brewing as she'd left the cabin. Not much of a storm then: some sleety drizzle and a little wind, and she'd thought nothing of it. Her chat with Mrs. Trapp had lasted a bit longer than she'd intended, but she'd excused herself in reasonable time and headed back for the cabin. Hurrying because the storm had suddenly picked up, sleet lashing in fierce spurts at her bare head. Quick alarm rose in her as, nearing the cabin, she saw the door hanging ajar and banging in the wind. *Gud bevara,* how could this happen? She'd made a point of securing the latch firmly.

Running inside, she'd almost stumbled over Jan. Face down on the floor, dead drunk and passed out. Returning before her, he'd either failed to close the door or had left the latch unfastened. Wind was caroming savagely around the room, drawn by hairline cracks in the old building, blasting sleety charges of cold and ice and wet over everything. But Sofie's eyes were all for the crib where Eric lay in his damp chill blankets and a whipping draft, coughing and crying. Crying for a mother who hadn't been there. That was all she could think as she'd stripped away damp bedding in a rush to make the child warm and dry. It was quickly done, and even in her weeping, angry dismay with herself and Jan, she hadn't felt fear. Not then, not yet.

Eric had quieted down, his coughing ebbed, he slept. Yet it was a twitching, restless sleep; his skin was touched by fever. So, worriedly, Sofie had stayed up by his crib all night. She'd left Jan where he was, snoring off his drunk on the floor, but a bitter resolve had burned in her mind. She would not live with such a man any longer. It had been bad enough with her father, a gentle-natured drunk. But this brute, this *gris!* He'd beaten her for the last time, but that was nothing to the endangering of his son's life. No. *Her* son. All hers now; she would take him away, anywhere that was far from Jan Ekstrom.

But Eric's fever had worsened during the night. By morning Sofie was in a near panic. As usual the Trapps had been helpful and solicitous, Cyrus sending a man to Saltville for the doctor, Adah insisting that the baby be moved to the big house again. And Sofie's long vigil had begun. Now she remembered the doctor's grim look and words. Croup. Grippe. Complications. The fever would build to a crisis; then they would know. But Sofie was sure she already knew. Her baby's life was slipping away, ebbing before her eyes as the hours wore on, and there was nothing she could do.

Again Adah was speaking with quiet insistence. "Sofie, listen to me. You must get some rest. If you're to be of any help to your baby . . ."

She turned the sense of these words sluggishly over in her mind. Yes. Mrs. Trapp was right. Only her twitching nerves were keeping her from sleep now. Sodden with exhaustion, she wasn't merely useless, she was a danger. Someone fresh and alert should keep the watch. She raised her eyes to Adah's.

"You call me if there is anything? You promise this?"

"Of course. You're being sensible now. My room is next to this one and you can rest there. Come along."

Unsteady, stumbling a little, she let Adah help her into the next room. The moment she hit the soft bed, her senses blacked away. She slept totally and dreamlessly.

Someone was shaking her by the shoulder. Sofie's mind fought stuporously against that imperative hand. She wanted only this warm fog of sleep. Then the shock of remembrance came; she sat up wildly.

"*Eric* —"

Adah stood there, her face stricken and help-less. She said nothing. There was no need. The look on her face said it. . . .

Sofie remembered little of afterward. She thought that she'd only been asleep for minutes, but Adah said no, she had slept for many hours, and during that time there had seemed no change in Eric's condition. She or Tula had stayed by him constantly. It was over very suddenly. One minute he still burned with fever. The next he was gone.

Sofie sat in the Ekstrom cabin by herself, not sure how she had gotten here, only that she'd insisted on being by herself. She shivered in the cold room. Thought of her shawl, but made no move to get it. Just sat and stared at the empty crib. She had not cried, she did not cry now. Her body and mind stayed strangely frozen.

The door creaked open. Cold air poured into the room and it roused her slightly. Then she saw Jan Ekstrom on the threshold. His face was ugly, furtive, bloated. He did not look at her. As he stumbled toward the bed, she smelled the heavy reek of whiskey.

She got slowly to her feet. Something broke in her like ice slivering to pieces. She began to tremble.

"Murderer!" She rushed suddenly at him, her

hands up and fisted. "Murderer, murderer, *murderer!*"

She beat crazily at the flushed smear of his face. He gave a hoarse cry and stumbled back to the door. She followed him, beating on his head and shoulders, screaming the word over and over. Then he was out the door and weaving blindly away across the yard.

Sofie sank down against the door, her weight pressing it shut. She dropped her forehead against the rough wood. "Murderer," she whispered. Then the grief spilled out of her in deep, wrenching sobs.

CHAPTER EIGHT

Cyrus felt tired to his bones as he slumped into his old swivel chair. He took off his neatly blocked Stetson and dropped it on the desk top, and stared at it. What the hell, he wondered, was the use of it all? He let his weary glance rove around his office and touch its familiar objects, finding no comfort in them. Life. What did it mean, if it meant anything? Hell. He was full up with living.

He couldn't remember feeling so depressed. He hadn't been able to refuse Mrs. Ekstrom's request that he say the words over her baby. He'd suggested sending for the circuit preacher, who was due in Saltville around now, but she wouldn't hear of it. She'd wanted Cyrus to say the words for the departed. He knew them well. Had said them before. How many times over the long years? For a daughter. A wife. Crewmen who had died in Chainlink's service and whose faces he no longer remembered. Most of them dead before their time, victims of a country that took its toll quickly and savagely, slowly and savagely. Always unmercifully.

Maybe you'll be the next, Cyrus thought. Maybe that was the thing. God, what had happened to his old vitality these last few weeks? Even the slow walk to the little cemetery back of the east ridge, walking behind Sofie Ekstrom and the small pine box in her arms, standing while two crewmen dug the grave, and the dreary walk back here, had left him feeling drained and useless. He felt a dull pain stir in his temples and gripped his knees, waiting. But the pain subsided. Sometimes it still did. A seldom thing these days without recourse to the needle.

Cyrus roused himself with a self-chiding grunt. He still had strength, and duties to perform while he had it. There'd be a time — but cross that bridge when it came up. He stretched his arms, swore mildly at the unaccustomed constrictions of a broadcloth suit, then shucked off the coat and swept his hat aside. Flipping open an account book, he scanned the figures. But it was hard to concentrate over the blurry spotting of his eyes which he couldn't — any longer — lay to a need for new glasses. Restively he swung his chair to face a window, clamping his jaws against his aches. A ride. Good long ride. Goddammit, why not? Hell with taking it easy. Hell with medical warnings that likely wouldn't stretch his time by a single day. Take that ride while he could. Might be his last.

He reached for his hat and was pushing out of his chair when someone knocked lightly at the outside door. Cyrus slacked back. "Come in," he growled.

Sofie Ekstrom entered. She closed the door and stood with her back to it. She had on the black dress she'd worn to the funeral. Her face was haggard, pale, numbly calm, as it had been ever since he'd first seen it after her baby's death night before last. But there was something else in it too. Something hard as glass that Cyrus sensed might shatter like glass. He glanced at the worn carpetbag she held before her, both hands clenched around the handle.

"What's this, now?"

"I am leaving. I want to thank you for your kindness, Mister Trapp, and I ask one more thing if it's not too much."

Cyrus stroked a finger along his jaw. "Leaving, eh? Kind of sudden, that."

"No. I think so before, even before —" She checked herself. "Don't, I ask you, try to stop me."

"Nobody'll stop you."

"Maybe you will have a man hitch a wagon and take me to Saltville. It is trouble, but I will give you no more."

"There's no trouble here you brought," Cyrus said dryly, quietly. "You just hold off a minute, Missus, and hear me out. You want to leave then, I will drive you in myself." Heaving himself from his chair, he paced a half-circle. He felt her eyes waiting; they wore a bright glaze that made him think of blue china scrubbed to a shine. Go easy now, he told himself.

"He still sleeping it off? Your husband?"

She didn't reply, which was answer enough. Ekstrom had stayed drunk all yesterday. She'd refused to remain in the shack with him and had spent the night in the big house.

"Where you plan to go? Back to Minnesota?"

"There is a railroad out of Saltville, eh?"

"Yeah, a spur line. Train comes there maybe twice a week. You'll have to lay over at the hotel. You got money?"

She was silent a moment. "I can find work in Saltville for a couple weeks maybe."

Cyrus's grunt expressed doubt. "You got people in Minnesota?"

"In Douglas County, neighbors — that were."

"No kin? A brother maybe? Sister?"

"No. There is nobody. I make my way. I have always."

"Maybe," Cyrus said gently, "you had better give it a little more time."

Sofie's clenched hands whitened at the knuckles. "Maybe you think I ever forgive what that man did?"

"All I'm thinking, it's not a thing to decide now."

"I will not live with him any more. Never."

"Nobody's all to blame for any one thing that happens. You lived long enough to know that, Sofie."

"It is not only this, there are other things." A nerve twitched in her cheek. "These you know nothing of."

Cyrus gave a weary nod. He hadn't failed to notice the bruises on her face from time to time. "All right. But take it slow. You can't go kiting off with no plans. There's a spare room upstairs. You go up and rest yourself. You can stay there or move back into the other place when he's gone."

"Gone?" Her eyes flickered. "You will make him go?"

"Up in the hills, sure. He can work a line job for awhile. Be out of your hair that long. Then we'll see. How long's he been this way? I mean the booze."

"It started when we came here," she said dully. "Never before."

"All right, give him a spell. There'll be no booze where he's going. Time and roughing it some'll take it out of his system."

"That will not change the man."

"You know that, eh? What's happened might."

"I don't know. I don't want to. . . ." Her voice trailed off. The bright edge of masked hysteria had faded; her face was dull and indifferent now. But docile.

"Thing is, you are going to wait. You're in no shape for thinking on what's to be done. How long since you had a good sleep? Go on up to the room and lay down." Cyrus tugged his beard, nodding a little. "Go on. You don't think about things any more for a spell, Missus. Then we'll talk again."

Bowie and Sully were on the lookout ledge above Yellow Pass when two riders came jogging across the humpy plains below the foothills. Bowie spotted them first and directed Sully's attention, pointing an arm as the half-breed trained his field glasses.

"Paleface got Injun eye," said Sully. "One's Cyrus. The other — damned if it ain't the Swenska."

"Ekstrom?"

They exchanged puzzled glances, then moved back off the ledge. They were waiting in the clearing where they'd located their dry cold camp as the horsemen, having ascended the ridge along the old game trail that led to its summit, gigged their mounts into view out of the trees.

Cyrus dismounted, growling, "Seems I caught you just sojering around in camp."

"Do tell," Sully said dryly. "We only spotted you about a half mile off. You come to take over the watch, you're welcome to it."

"You wouldn't be that lucky. I only brought you some company." Cyrus came over to them, rubbing his big hands briskly together. "*Is* cold up here, ain't it?"

"I'm surprised you noticed," Sully said sardonically.

Standing in front of them now, Cyrus lowered his voice. "The Swede's in a bad way. His baby is dead."

Both men just looked at him, then Sully said quietly, "Christ." They watched Ekstrom drop heavily out of his saddle and stand with his head sunk between his hunched shoulders. His face was blotched and puffy and sick-looking.

"It's a bad thing," Cyrus said grimly. He told them briefly what had happened. "Don't know if

121

it's the best thing to bring him up here, but couldn't think of no better. Either of you got any booze in your possibles, I want you to get rid of it."

"We had any redeye on hand," Sully said dourly, "it would of disappeared a good while back."

Cyrus grunted. "Want you men to keep an eye on the Swede. Keep him busy if you can." He motioned at the pack horse. "Brought you some more grub. I take it nothing's happened."

"Nary sign of a long-looper," Sully said. "We been wondering if they got wind of us some way. Don't see how, though. We been following your orders. No fire, no shooting. So there's no word on vented cattle being put up for sale."

Cyrus shook his head. "Maybe those jacklegs quit the raids, but they got to be holding the cattle somewhere. Maybe back in the brush till spring comes. In that case, no use leaving you boys sitting up here till your asses freeze."

"We been wondering if that might occur to you."

"Well, I did allow how tender your sensibilities are. Keep the watch a few more days, then we'll see. Unload the pack horse, Sully, and tell Ekstrom to help you." Sully looked dubious, and Cyrus said: "He'll take your orders right enough. He is acting kind of strange, but that should wear off. Just don't let him sit around and don't pamper him."

Sully walked over to Ekstrom and spoke to

him. Without a word the Swede turned to the pack horse, bracing the tarp-wrapped supplies on its back while Sully loosened the diamond hitch. Cyrus watched a moment, then turned to Bowie. "Come along, Candler. Want to see your lookout."

Bowie tramped ahead, leading the way through some scrub trees. They stepped out on the flat spur of rock jutting above the pass. Wind cut icily at their faces: sunlight touching the peaks belied the chill of this late fall day. Cyrus stood with hands rammed in his mackinaw pockets, gazing into the pass.

"Nice view from here. Ain't been up on this rim in years."

"You ought to squat on it for a week some time," Bowie told him.

Cyrus grinned. Bowie thought that he looked definitely older, strangely tired, as if some part of him had burned out. And Cyrus's next words, quiet and abrupt, surprised him.

"How old are you, Candler?"

"Crowding thirty-seven."

"Hell, you're just touching the prime years. You a native Texan?"

"You mean was I born there, no. Georgia."

"Huh. How you come by a good Texican name like Bowie?"

"Same reason my two older brothers got named Houston and Crockett. Pap got to Texas just once, in the Mexican War."

Cyrus seemed to be in a talkative way. Bowie

felt a difference in him that went deeper than surface. His manner was reflective, sort of; his gaze seemed weary and far away. In answer to his questions, Bowie said that his Pap had always wanted to return to Texas one day, but had never made it. There'd been a farm, a wife and kids, a life of hardscrabble drudgery just to make ends meet.

"Sounds like your pa kept that one dream alive," Cyrus said musingly. "Man does that. He needs a dream."

"Pap died at forty-five," Bowie said tonelessly. "Milk sickness took Ma when I was two. Dreams didn't do old Pap a lick of good."

"You're wrong, Candler. Just one good dream is what keeps a man going. Me, I made mine a reality right enough, but I still say the struggle was the best of it."

"Easy to say when a man's made his."

"Easy, hell," Cyrus growled. "I was damn near thirty before I got started on mine. Had made good money selling broncs I caught and rough-busted till my bones lost their green. Man gets his fill of cracked ribs and busted fingers. Maybe I had one edge, but it sure-hell didn't seem like one at the time. I'd a been a spending fool except that I couldn't go see the elephant like the other boys done. So I saved up."

Bowie eyed him. "What edge?"

"I couldn't take spirits."

"Come again?"

"Few swigs of tanglefoot'd turn me into a wild

124

man. That was my edge. I'd become a damn lunatic, a holy terror. Time was mothers kept their kids offen the streets when they heard Cyrus Trapp was in town. Well —" Cyrus took his hands from his pockets and held them open. "Happen I finally killed a man with these. That's when I swore off for good. Turned out best for me, all right, but that never helped the poor bastard I beat to death. Whatever you get in this life, boy, you pay for. One way or the other, you pay."

"So it don't hardly seem worth it."

"That's bullshit," Cyrus said flatly. "Near got thinking that way myself, and it's bullshit. Just as long as a man can keep the candle going is worth it. Only —" He shoved his hands back in his pockets and squinted across the valley. "A man wants to leave something behind him too."

"I'd say you're leaving a hell of a lot."

Cyrus jerked out a dry chuckle. "Sure. Land, maybe? The land was here before I set eyes on it. All I got is paper to show tenancy, you might say. Buildings, cattle, money? Couple sons to leave it all to? A wife? Adah can't run Chainlink. All I can leave her is enough money to see she'll be comfortably off. And I can tell you right now that when I'm gone, Adah will go back to the city. Joe-Bob can't take hold. And Brady, it'll run through his fingers like sand."

"You're talking like you —"

Cyrus's gaze sharpened on him, and Bowie broke off.

125

"Like I might be gone tomorrow?" Cyrus grinned mirthlessly. "The boys in the bunkhouse been speculating, have they? Well, that's the fact of it, Candler. You're a close-mouthed sort; you won't be needing to pass any of this on." He hunched his shoulders as if against a deeper chill than the biting wind. "There's a thing growing on my brain. Have got the pain checked for now. Laudanum, opiate hypodermics. But I look to go hard when the time comes. Maybe I won't wait for it. No telling what a man will do, come to that."

Bowie didn't know what to say, and after a moment Cyrus went on: "Maybe it all evens out somewhere. A man likes to think so. There's a lot to think on when his time comes. My boys, now. Maybe I was too hard on 'em when they was tads. Expected more'n they could give and whipped their asses raw when they couldn't match up. Now — maybe I gone way too soft, like Brady says. Happens when a man comes to look for peace with himself." He turned his glance full on Bowie. "It don't shine much when a man's alone, Candler."

Bowie shrugged. "You got to choose for yourself, I reckon."

"You think you do. Always figured a man makes his chances. Always lived by that thought. But a man alone don't stand a chance. Remember what I say." He looked away. "Woman to share with is a pleasant thing. But not one with different ways. Not one half your age either.

It don't work worth a damn."

Cyrus fell silent, staring across the valley as if drinking it in for the last time. Then he turned and tramped back to the clearing, and Bowie followed. Cyrus took Sully aside now; they conversed for some minutes, and then Cyrus motioned Bowie over.

"If anything breaks," he told them, "you boys send Ekstrom back with word. You two take care of any rough doings. I'm thinking of his wife."

Sully glanced at Bowie, then said casually, "How's she bearing up?"

"She wanted to leave him. Leave Chainlink. I made her see that idea wasn't for the best on her own account, but rest of it's up to Ekstrom. If we can fetch him back dry and straightened up some'at, it'll be worth it."

"Sure," Sully said.

They watched Cyrus mount and ride away into the trees. Thinking back on their talk, Bowie felt only a little puzzled. Cyrus had some private words for Sully too, but Bowie had already concluded that Sully was more of a son to him than his own sons. Speaking frankly with a pilgrim he hardly knew was something else. Yet thinking it over, Bowie realized it wasn't so strange after all. For this had been a lonely man telling his feelings to a man who could take something kindred from his words. *Remember what I say,* Cyrus had said. And Bowie knew he would.

127

Before the day was out, Ekstrom was completely sobered. The high chill air was a crisp bracer to his whiskey-shot system. But it didn't improve his disposition by a jot. Earlier he had dulled the savage edge of his remorse with drinking. As he began rousing from his lethargy, he was a man brooding and balky and trigger-tempered.

Bowie got the first hint of trouble to come when he took Ekstrom with him to the place where he and Sully had been cooking their grub, a sheltered back canyon some distance from Yellow Pass. Bowie began laying out the grub by the ashes of an old fire while the Swede stood by making no move to help, a sulky blond bear of a man who glowered in silence.

"We need wood," Bowie told him. "Make yourself useful. There's some dead brush down the canyon a ways."

"You think I'm your goddam servant?" Ekstrom growled. It was the first thing he'd said all day.

Bowie straightened up, watching him. "We're up here to do a job," he said quietly. "You do your part, that's all."

He thought for a moment that Ekstrom was going to crowd it here and now. He'd seen the same hair-trigger look in other boozeheads suddenly cut off from the means to feed their craving. Compound that with a naturally surly man freighted by guilt and you might have a wildcat by the tail. Bowie could make allowances for Ekstrom's state of mind, but he was ready for anything that might happen.

Maybe Ekstrom saw it. After a moment he turned to his horse. Bowie said, "You can fetch it better on foot," but Ekstrom ignored him, swinging into his saddle. He flung the animal around on a brutal rein and kicked him into motion up the rocky floor of the canyon. Bowie shook his head, then bent back to his task. Laying a slab of bacon on a flat rock, he hacked off strips and laid them in a skillet. He half-filled a Dutch oven at a spring that bubbled up through rocks nearby. As he was opening a sack of pinto beans, he heard the shot. Its echoes clapped wildly up and down the wooded slopes of the canyon.

Bowie muttered, "Jesus," and loped over to Shitkicker. Mounting, he heeled the buckskin into a hard trot up the gorge. Angling around a bend, he came on Ekstrom's mount with the reins trailing. No sign of the Swede.

"Ekstrom!"

A rustling in the dense oak scrub that cloaked the south slope. The Swede came tramping into sight, his saddle gun swinging from his fist.

"What the hell was that shooting?"

"I got a deer."

Bowie stared at him a moment, then swung to the ground. "Where'd you drop it?"

Ekstrom wore a look of sullen vindication. He pointed. Bowie went past him and rammed through the thickets going upslope. Easy to pick up the trail of broken twigs and blood-splashed leaves where the mortally hit animal had bounded away. Bowie followed it a few yards to where the deer, a small doe, had dropped in the graceless sprawl of death. Ekstrom came tramping up beside him.

"We didn't need the meat," Bowie said thinly.

Ekstrom shrugged. "All Trapp said, no shooting close to the Pass."

"There was no damn need."

Ekstrom eyed him with a sultry arrogance. "Shit. It is just a deer. There's plenty deer around here, tracks all over. If there's trouble to come, maybe I need the practice, eh?"

"God damn a man that kills game and then leaves it to rot." Bowie spoke with deceptive softness, but couldn't keep the shaking from his voice. "You're going to skin this carcass and cut it up. Then you're going to pack the meat back to camp."

"Like hell I —"

Bowie moved almost before the words were out, grabbing the barrel of Ekstrom's carbine and twisting upward. Ekstrom tightened his grasp too late. Bowie wrenched the weapon away and swung it in a tight arc, slamming the breech against Ekstrom's jaw. The teeth-rattling clout knocked him backward, stumbling. He caught his balance and stood rubbing his jaw.

"You son of a bitch. I kill you for that."

Bowie swung his arm and let go of the carbine,

spinning it away into the brush. He settled his weight on the balls of his feet, waiting. Ekstrom did not move. Bowie reached inside his mackinaw now, pulled his knife from its sheath and gave it a hard flip that drove the blade into the loam at Ekstrom's feet.

"Use it. The deer or me. It's your choice."

Ekstrom bent slowly and picked up the knife. Bowie watched him contemptuously, thinking it was no gamble at all. Though he wasn't altogether sure. Not until Ekstrom shook himself and let his yellow-eyed glance slip away. Wordlessly, then, he knelt by the deer and began skinning it out.

CHAPTER NINE

Leaving Ekstrom to butcher the doe, Bowie gathered an armload of wood and returned down canyon. He took the Swede's carbine with him. He had finished cooking up the grub when Ekstrom came trudging into sight leading his horse, the deer's hide slung from its back and bulging with the saddle and quarters of venison. His clothes were stained with blood and slimy fluids. Bowie didn't have to check the meat to know that he'd botched the job of butchering. There was raw hatred in Ekstrom's look, and now Bowie wondered if he'd crowded too hard. This was a man already crowded to a savage edge by grief and guilt and a cold-turkey cut-off of his habit. Salted by a streak of plain damn meanness. A good thing he'd taken the gun away, Bowie decided.

They packed the grub and meat back to camp. Bowie told Ekstrom to hang the venison from a tree limb for a night's cooling. While the Swede was occupied with that, he quietly told Sully what had happened. Sully shook his head. "Verily, I believe you grabbed the bull by the balls there, paleface."

"What would you of done?"

"Hell. Somewhat the same, I reckon. But I don't like his look a damn bit. He was riding grudge on you before. Makes it worse."

Bowie said flatly: "You want to enlarge on that?"

"You want me to?"

"Don't hedge with me, boy."

"Well, when you was looking to that baby's well-being, talking with Miz Ekstrom now and again, some of the boys taken it you was shining to her. Ekstrom got wind of what somebody said and blew up over it."

"That kind of talk could get somebody killed," Bowie said thinly.

"That's what I figured. You wasn't about when it happened and I didn't see a need you should know."

"Thanks."

"Look, you can get pretty damn redheaded yourself. Seemed best to let it lay. Hell, I knew they was cutting wrong sign on you, but Ekstrom didn't. I caught him looking knives at you a couple times after. So watch yourself."

Next morning they peered out of their pine-bough shelter to find the weather a little warmer than usual and a wet fog blanketing everything. It had turned the bottom of Yellow Pass to a misty void, but that didn't matter a lot; sounds of riders or cattle going between its stony walls would be easily picked up. Ekstrom was the big problem. He seemed to have worsened over-night. He went mechanically about the tasks he was assigned muttering continually to himself, his bloodshot eyes glassy and glaring. As if he were squeezing every atom of his desperate rage

133

into a bombshell that might go off any time. Bowie took Sully aside; they talked.

"I dunno," Sully said soberly. "Am beginning to think he ain't altogether right in the head. But we got orders."

"Orders be damned," Bowie said. "One of us is got to take him back to headquarters. This job is a bitch as it is. Having a man who's sick or crazy dragging about waiting a chance to put a bullet or a knife in me is cutting it too damn fine."

"Well, I do appreciate it's your hide, white brother. All right, you keep the watch. I'll ride back with him today. Tell Cyrus how it is."

Their supply of water was low and the nearest place to get more was from a spring at the base of this same ridge a few hundred yards east. It was Bowie's turn to fetch it. With two wooden buckets swinging from his fists, he set off down the old trail and, coming to the ridge base, headed eastward parallel to it. Great rocks that had fallen from the steeper faces of the ridge littered the ground, half-seen shapes in the milky shroud of fog.

Bowie reached the spring, which pooled in a deep trough below where it cascaded from the lower slope. He was kneeling to dip the buckets when the shot came. It followed the whine and snap of a slug that spattered rock particles head-level from a boulder to his right.

Jesus!

Bowie dived sideways and flattened out on his

belly, twisting his head around for a look. He saw a man's figure dodge from one rock to the next, clutching a saddle gun. Just a gray silhouette briefly seen, but its heavy shape was easy to identify. Ekstrom had followed him here. Bowie hugged the earth, heart pounding. He hadn't packed his pistol along, but Ekstrom wasn't sure of that or he'd be coming on straight and fast to cinch his kill.

What had happened to Sully? Bowie hadn't heard a shot; Ekstrom might have put Sully out of action some other way. So here he was, unarmed, within a minute or so of having bought it unless he could get away from Ekstrom. It was all open flats down here, the ridge too steep to scale at this point. The rocks and fog offered the only hope of covering an escape.

Lunging to his feet, Bowie piled into a crouching run toward a belt of tall boulders. Another shot sent flinty echoes caroming across the rock field and now Ekstrom lifted his voice in a bawl of rage. A fragment of rock turned under Bowie's right foot; in his driving run he skidded sideways, then plowed on his shoulder into the stony ground.

He tried to get his feet under him. Pain stabbed his ankle and he fell to his hands and knees. Ekstrom's boots crunched over the flints as he came on at a run, his fog-grayed form looming darker and larger by the moment. Suddenly he was close, pulling to a stop.

He laughed as he levered his carbine and

threw it to his shoulder.

Bowie had lurched to his feet, but he was helpless to do anything except brace for the slug's impact. His body shrank with the slam and grunt, the echo of gun blast. But it was Ekstrom who was hammered forward by the shot, falling, his arms flung wide. He struck the ground in a broken sprawl and didn't move.

Bowie had often seen game go down hard-hit; he knew Ekstrom wouldn't move again. His stomach pitching hollowly, he stumbled over to the dead man. His eyes moved to Sully as he came tramping through the rocks, rifle in hand. He and Bowie reached the body at the same time. Sully knelt and turned it over and said bleakly: "Well, he had to buy it all. The sorry goddam fool."

"Thought he might of got you some ways."

Sully shook his head tightly. "He sneaked off. Told him to throw his stuff together while I fetched the horses. Didn't take much to figure I meant to fetch him back — directly I was gone, he found his carbine and skinned out after you. I found him gone, all I could do was follow fast as I could. But Christ. Who'd a thought he'd go off a-sudden like this, like a goddam string of Chinese firecrackers?"

"Nobody," Bowie said. "You done what had to be."

A shudder ran through Sully. "Jesus. I guess I did. I'll pack him to headquarters and tell what happened. My job."

"Wonder if we couldn't cover what happened. Bury him here, give out a different story. Say he got killed in an accident. Be a sight easier on his wife."

"Yeah." Sully rubbed his chin. "Only any story we give out'll look goddam funny. Cyrus might go along with us, but then he'd have to explain unusual circumstances of death to the sheriff. Coroner'll have to see the body, hold an inquest. Let's take a day and night to think on it. He'll keep."

"All right."

"How's that foot?"

Bowie tested part of his weight on it. "Hurts like hell. Pulled something, but I can hobble. You better pack him up to camp."

The fog got thicker as the day wore on; its wetness sheened like dull pearl on rocks and trees. The chill moisture worked under Bowie's slicker and into his flesh as he crouched on the lookout ledge. He and Sully had reached no conclusions on how to handle the telling of Ekstrom's death. It made no difference except on Sofie Ekstrom's account, and Bowie drowsily wondered if she'd care all that much. Even allowing that Ekstrom might once have been a good husband in his way, it seemed unlikely that feeling had ever run deep between them. Too many differences. Ekstrom had been older than Sofie by perhaps fifteen years, but that wouldn't mean so much; it wasn't too great an age gap. Bowie sleepily reflected that he was a good dozen years older than her himself. . . .

He was half-dozing when the faint noises first reached him. Then he snapped to alertness. Muffled sounds of cattle on the move. A good-sized bunch. And very faintly, men's voices hoorawing from hoarse throats. Bowie strained his eyes against the pale broth of mist. The pass below was a foggy gulf; only a growing nearness in the sounds indicated that the cattle were being funneled into its mouth. The voices grew louder and sharper.

At last. And about time, by God.

Bowie got stiffly to his feet and returned to the camp at a limping trot. Shaking Sully by the shoulder roused him out of his damp blankets. They hustled to fetch their horses. "Christ, they picked a night for it," Sully grumbled as he threw on his saddle, but a rising excitement tinged his voice. Bowie allowed that more likely the night had picked them; it would be no picnic to haze off stock in this murk. The fog would also make good cover for anyone trailing them.

The two Chainlink men picked their way down the ridge trail and, once they achieved the bottom, swung in a short arc to enter the V-shaped cleft of Yellow Pass. The rustlers would have a slow time of it, chousing their beeves through this tight defile. Bowie and Sully were careful to hold well to their rear, keeping the distance by ear. Though the floor of the pass stayed at a generally uniform breadth, in some places the walls above cramped almost together in sheer drops of a hundred and more feet from bulging crags of rimrock. Men's voices, gravelly from shouting, drifted a surprising distance down the gorge.

The canyon flanks began to taper low. Finally they dwindled away altogether. The trail continued to follow the dry bed of the ancient stream that had carved out Yellow Pass centuries before. Dense gouts of fog made it hard to tell much else about the country they were crossing. It was strewn with huge boulders that materialized from the mist and receded into it; occasional crooked leafless trees thrust up like crabbed skeletons. You had the eerie feeling of crossing the face of a dead world. Good place for a drive-off, all right; you'd be hard put to pick up cold track on this sort of terrain. At the same time, sounds of cattle on the move carried sharply here and were easy to follow.

Soon the trail left the old stream bed and bent roughly northeast, threading circuitously around rugged heights of land. The raiders kept up a steady pace, completely sure of their route despite the fog. Twice Bowie caught a purling of water ahead and each time the trail crossed wide shallow streams or, what seemed more likely, different crooks of the same stream. And each time the cattle were driven a distance upstream through foot-deep water before they were pushed up the opposite bank. Cyrus had been right, Bowie thought; the best trackers trying to pick up this trail later might be confused any number of places.

The night hours crawled by; the fog began to lift. But as it cleared, its wetness dissolved into a mizzling rain. The damp cold increased. Rocking at this held-in pace, Bowie felt familiar cramps ease into his joints. He had to continuously flex his legs and arms, toes and fingers, to keep them from going numb. What miserable goddam weather to dog out a slow trail.

The land was starting to climb perceptibly; the rocky scape gave way to patches of turf and occasional mottes of the lodgepole pine that forested much of this high country. The trees were stunted and gnurled at first, growing taller and straighter as the trail climbed. The loam underfoot was spongy pine detritus which, like rocks and water, left practically no sign. Except for the old or fresh cattle droppings here and there. A flare of gray light rimmed along a forested swell of ridge to their right. Real dawn was still hours away, but the night was starting to heel off. With the visibility improving, Bowie and Sully began to catch occasional glimpses of the raiders and the bunched cattle. Accordingly they dropped farther behind.

The land continued to climb, but just ahead it seemed to fall sharply away. Cattle and men showed on the paling skyline and then they dropped out of sight. When Bowie and Sully reached the same spot, they found themselves at the head of a long slide of collapsed shale down which the cattle had been driven. It had crumbled long ago from the rimrock of a short sheer cliff, forming a kind of uneven ramp to the floor of a rich-grassed valley.

The bowl-shaped depression was several hundred feet across, irregularly oval in shape, and hedged around by natural barriers of crumbling shale walls and thick stands of lodgepole. The meadow of wild hay was dotted by giant isolated pines and rambling clots of brush, giving the valley a parklike appearance. A growing band of light showed bunches of cattle dark against the sun-cured grass.

"You feel heroic, any?" Sully murmured.

"I feel like a froze jackass," Bowie growled, watching the men haze the Chainlink cattle deep into the valley. "I count six riders. More than we figured on. I vote we take word back to headquarters."

"Yours is the speech of gray hairs, brother. Take us a whole day to reach headquarters and fetch men back here."

"Christ, boy. You think these cows are going to stray some'eres?"

"Men might. They likely be gone when we get back. Paleface, we waited many suns to catch these jacklegs in the act. Getting the cattle back won't satisfy Cyrus if we lose the men."

"So we just take on all six."

A reckless glint touched Sully's glance. "No harm in waiting to see what they do next, is there? Might show us a way to handle 'em. You can't tell."

Bowie thought it was a piece of damn foolishness, but he conceded there was no harm in watching a while. Just that he had no intention of sticking his neck out against odds. The misting rain held a bite of sleet now; he shivered and dug his chin deep in his collar. The raiders were showing no disposition to leave yet. After dispersing the cattle, they rode to a sheltering motte of pines and dropped out of their saddles. Soon a spot of fiery orange showed at the edge of timber. They were going to warm themselves anyway.

"Listen," Sully said now, "why'n't we sneak down there? Go in on foot. If we can't take 'em, we might get close enough to identify 'em. The law likes a couple witnesses, doesn't it?"

"Yeah."

Bowie's growl held a resigned note. But feeling the taste of high excitement himself, he knew that he was of Sully's mind. They had waited out a long hard stand for this time; that should give a man some rights. Maybe, just maybe, they could bring it off.

Leaving their horses back in some trees, carrying their saddle guns, the two descended the slide and worked cautiously toward the fire. Fading darkness still offered some cover; it was easy to conceal their approach by holding behind the fingers of brush that laced the valley floor. In a short time they were hunkered down in a patch of chokecherry scrub a couple hundred feet from the fire. Its glow picked the gang out clearly. They were passing around a bottle. Bowie couldn't identify any of them until one, a bulky figure of a man, turned against the throw of flame-light. It caught on his face.

Brady Trapp. A moment later Bowie recognized a slighter figure that was Joe-Bob.

Sully said in a shocked whisper: "You make out what I do?"

"I make out the Trapps are helping steal their old man's beef. I don't make sense of it."

Neither did Sully. He quickly named two of the others. The tall brick-haired man was Red Antrim; one sallow puffy-faced weed of a fellow was called Blue Searls. "Don't know that other pair, but Searls is one of Red's cross-dog outfit."

"Seems they're the rest of it."

"Uh-huh."

They continued to watch. Needles of sleet rattled on their hatbrims; wind curled fiercely off the heights. It blew the fire to yellow tatters and carried snatches of talk. Apparently Brady and Antrim were debating whether or not to head the cattle toward market now or wait out the bad weather. Brady was impatient, chafing against delay, arguing that the sleet might be followed by heavy snow, stranding the cattle here till spring and risking their loss. Antrim acknowledged the danger, but he was more concerned about the cattle getting bogged down by a snowstorm in the rugged country between here and

Craigie; at least the cattle were sheltered here. The talk grew heated. Meantime the bottle had been emptied. Another was broken out and passed from man to man.

Antrim appeared to have won the point. Brady retreated into surly silence, settling on his heels by the fire and gazing into it. Antrim's men were getting louder as their innards warmed. One of them threw the empty bottle high in the air and all three blazed away at it with pistols, whooping. Nobody hit it. Antrim grouchily told them to lay off the goddam racket.

"Brother," Sully whispered, "if we gonna to make the move, best we do it before it gets any lighter. Three of 'em are hooched up and that Joe-Bob, he'll be no trouble."

"All right. We better split apart, take 'em from two sides."

"Yeah. You stay here, I'll circle onto the other flank. Will sing out when I am set. Too bad we can't run off the horses, but they're too close to 'em." Sully's teeth flashed. "Injun always go after horse first."

"So I heard. When you sing out, see you give 'em a chance to give up."

"Why, yes. Honest to Great Spirit, o white brother, Sully is not one of your murdering savages."

Bowie grunted. "Sure, sure. Get moving."

Sully slipped away through the straggling thickets, vanishing among them in utter silence. Bowie crouched with his rifle across his knees, putting all his attention on the camp. His tendon-pulled ankle ached steadily. Antrim kept pacing up and down, as nervous in his way as Brady. Sometimes he hauled up and peered out at the valley, sometimes in Bowie's direction. That's a tough old lobo, Bowie thought. Did he really suspect something amiss? Hard to say. He wasn't one easily caught off balance, that was sure.

The seconds grew into long aching minutes. Or maybe he only imagined they did. What the hell was taking Sully so long?

Bowie was almost startled when the half-breed's order rang out: "Hold it like you are. This camp is surrounded!"

In an instant every man was on his feet, facing around toward the voice. Bowie rose swiftly to his feet and levered his rifle, stepping out to the open. "Shuck your guns," he called. "Any man of you bats a winker, he is done —"

Antrim wheeled like a catamount, palming up his side gun. Bowie's shot merged with Sully's. Antrim spun like a lanky dervish and then crashed across the fire, his body whipping up a shower of sparks. Another man had already dived for his rifle where it leaned against a deadfall. Bowie, levering fast, squeezed off a second shot. It took the man between the shoulder blades and slammed him against the deadfall like a broken doll.

Searls, his pistol out, had snapped two shots at Bowie. Mindful of the range then, he lunged for a horse and the rifle scabbarded on its saddle. Just then Sully stepped out to view, pistol leveled, and shot him in the leg. As Searls fell with a scream, Sully was turning the drop on Brady, who stood uncertainly, his gun half drawn.

"Try it," Sully invited.

Brady raised his hands. Antrim's third man hadn't moved a muscle after Sully's first order. He stood exactly as he'd been, holding his arms away from his body. Bowie came tramping up. "Take their hardware, Sully," he said. Sully moved from one man to the next, collecting guns and knives. Bowie glanced at the smoking fire half-smothered by Antrim's body; his clothes were smoldering.

"Pull him off," Bowie told the man who hadn't moved.

The fellow's eyes were like muddy ice, cold and wise. Wordlessly he walked to Antrim, grabbed him by the boots, and dragged him away from the fire. Joe-Bob hadn't moved either. Just stood looking on, round-eyed. Now he made an inarticulate sound, shaking his head.

"Oh, it's happening, all right," Sully said gently. "You got done to death by two men, boys."

Searls heaved himself from his belly onto his back with a screech of pain. His face was bloodless. "Jesus God —" He clutched at his leg. "Arch, Christ, I'm bleeding to death!"

Sully said: "Bleed, you cow-lifting bastard."

146

"You." Bowie tipped his rifle at the cold-eyed man. "Fix him up."

Sully raised his brows, then shrugged. The one called Arch said meagerly, "Need a knife." Bowie nodded at Sully, who handed Arch back his hunting knife. He kneeled by Searls and ripped open his pants leg.

Sully's dark glance shuttled to Brady. "You got some tall medicine to make, big brother."

"What you going to do?" Brady said huskily.

"Depends how good you talk." Bowie kicked up the fire. "I'm tracking some sign on you, Junior. You tell me if it's right. If Antrim's bunch vented the brands and then tried peddling the cows, they'd be ass-deep in trouble. So you got hand-picked to do the mischief. No need to vent brands."

Brady's face looked fishgut gray. He nodded. "My part was to sign the bill of lading at rail-head."

"As a Trapp representing his pa's outfit, eh? You're a real bucko lad, Junior. Your pa's cattle. You must need money damn bad."

"For that big new gambling debt he run up," Sully put in. "I know about it, Brady. Reckon everyone does but Cyrus."

"I was supposed to get a third," Brady muttered. "It would of cleared my debt."

"That's too bad," Bowie said. "That debt ain't half your problem."

"Goddammit, if you gonna take me in, go ahead. If you gonna shoot, do it! You got the chance." Brady added with a guttural ugliness, "That would suit you, ridgerunner."

"Sure," Bowie said. "Suppose you tell us all about it, Junior. Then I'll tell you what suits me."

Brady talked in a weary, strangled voice. Antrim had a contact at Craigie, a buyer who would take on wet cattle and ask no questions. The legitimacy of the transaction would be checked out by stockyard officials; with a bill of lading signed by Brady, the buyer would have no difficulty passing Chainlink cattle off at the yards. Antrim had slacked off some after that first quick flurry of raids and waited on word from Brady, surmising that Cyrus would take some counteraction. When Brady had reported that apparently Cyrus had no such plans under way, Antrim had gone ahead with a last big raid, tonight's. They'd throw these cattle in with their previous pickings, then trail the whole herd north to Craigie. Antrim had already meticulously scouted a good trail north through the Breaks. One hard push, trailing the herd day and night, and the stolen beeves would be off their hands.

"How come you and Joe-Bob was with Antrim's crowd tonight?" asked Sully.

Brady said that Antrim had needed a couple extra men for this last big strike and the drive to Craigie; Brady had offered his services and had taken Joe-Bob into his confidence to fill out the crew. They'd be gone from Chainlink a few days, but a ready-sounding story that they'd gone on a drunk in Saltville would cover their absence. Cyrus would rant about it later, but wouldn't have cause to doubt the story.

"All right, Junior," said Bowie. "Now I'll tell you what suits me." Bowie glanced at Sully. "It's got to suit you too."

Sully cocked a brow. "I don't make out your sign, paleface. What's to suit? We take the lot in."

"Listen," Brady argued, "no reason you can't let the kid go and not tell Cyrus, is there? Hell, he ain't done nothing. He come with me tonight, but he ain't really in it, he didn't know about it before."

Bowie didn't even look at him. "Stop and think a minute, Sully. How's old man Trapp going to take this?"

"Hell—" Sully shook his head. "It'll break the old man's heart, I suppose. He'll never bat an eye to show it, but I know him. Don't make a whit of difference what manner of pups he sired. They're his own. Ain't nothing changes a blood feeling and Cyrus has got the feeling deep in his guts."

"That's what I figured."

Sully looked slightly incredulous. "You saying we should let these Trapps go scot-free — say nothing to Cyrus?"

"That's about it. Ain't a case of liking to. Lesser of two evils, I reckon."

"Forgetting something, ain't you?" Sully gestured at Searls and Arch. "They got no reason not to tell the sheriff everything."

"And no good reason to, if they're turned loose. Every reason not to."

Sully was silent a moment, scowling as he digested the thought. Mizzle hissed on the coals. "Might be a better way," he said then. "Way to make sure. They're scum. Nobody'd question it much if it happened they got killed in the shoot-out."

"No," Bowie said flatly, promptly. "It's my way or no way." His eyes narrowed on Sully's. "Could you do that?"

Sully sighed and shook his head. "Come down to it, I reckon not. Just pitching pennies."

Bowie's glance slid back to Searls and Arch. "You hear what I'm saying?"

"Sure," Arch said softly.

"Searls?"

Searls raised his face. It was contorted and glistening; he kept fighting back squeaks of pain. He managed a nod.

"You cauterize his leg," Bowie told Arch. "We'll hold him for you. Then you'll help us bury your partners. Then you both get clear away from here. Our story will be you made a clean escape — in case the sheriff checks on who-all got buried here. You can make camp somewhere till Searls is fit to ride. When he is, you both clear the hell out of this country. Way out. Don't show your faces hereabouts again. You got that?"

"Sure," Arch murmured. "I got it, mister."

"There's just one thing." Sully moved over to Brady and wrapped a fist around the front folds of his slicker. "I want you to cinch onto something, big noise. It's on your pa's account you're walking away from the biggest jackpot of your life. But get this. From here on you are going to tread the straight and narrow. Cyrus ain't got a lot of time, but for what he's got, you are going to be a son of sorts. I'll be watching."

He dropped his fist and stepped back, his flat-lidded eyes fixing Brady's face. "You slip just once for that old man to see, and I'll make you the sorriest snake on two legs."

CHAPTER TEN

The yard was a chocolate-colored mire as Bowie slogged across it, his head bent against the gusts of sleety rain. Every step balled his boot soles with more gumbo, throwing him off balance, but he couldn't even dredge up the will to curse. He was dog-tired right to his guts, his ankle still hurt; he wanted nothing more than to collapse in his bunk and sleep the clock around, as Cyrus had ordered. But utterly spent as he was, he didn't think he could catch a wink till he'd gotten this errand over. It wasn't a welcome one; it just had to be done. And he grimly reckoned that it was his to do.

The windows of the Ekstrom cabin showed lamplight against the gray darkness of this late afternoon. He reached the door and paused to scrape his boots awkwardly on the sill, knocking off the mud. The noise brought Sofie Ekstrom to the door; she opened it.

"What is — oh, Mr. Candler."

"Yes'm. Could I come in?"

"*Ja*, of course. Here, let me take the coat and hat. *Himmel*, what weather it is."

Bowie moved into the room, shucking out of his slicker. "Yes'm. Can't stay but a minute."

"Come by the fire. I fix coffee."

He crossed to the fireplace, where a cheery blaze was going and held his hands to its warmth. He didn't quite know how to approach something of this sort. He'd never had to do the like. He glanced at Sofie as she poured water in a blackened coffeepot, ladled in Arbuckle's, and came over to slip the pot bail onto a fireplace lug. Her face was calm and pleasant; if she was grieving, it didn't show.

"Um, Miz Ekstrom, we took up a collection at the bunkhouse." He dug in the pocket of his duck jacket and pulled out a wad of greenbacks and held it out. "This is for you."

Sofie straightened, gazed at the money, then raised her eyes to his. "What is this for?"

"Well, it's something we do when a man dies on the job. If he leaves kin, wife or kids or maybe old folks, we get up some money for 'em."

She shook her head once, stiffly. "I cannot take money, Mr. Candler."

"Well, sure, but it's a custom, like. It's the right thing to do." He thrust the bills at her half awkwardly, half roughly. "You take it. It's from all of us. All the boys want you to have it."

Still she made no move to accept it. Bowie laid the money on the table. Slowly then, she picked it up. "It is so much." She began to blink and bite her underlip. *"Gad valingne def,"* she whispered. "God bless you — all of you."

Bowie nodded uncomfortably. "I better be going."

"No, please, you have coffee first. It is ready soon." She pressed the bills between her hands; tears began spilling from her eyes. *"Tack —*

thank you." She was crying, but she was smiling too, trying to fight the tears. "Thank you. Sit down, please, don't mind me."

Bowie slacked into a heavy carved chair. He looked at the fire. A few snifflings and she seemed to perk right up, hurrying back and forth from cupboard to table, setting out cups and spoons. It wasn't unpleasant to sit like this and soak up the warmth and listen to her movements, and he felt faintly guilty. He hadn't a notion what she might be feeling. No grief, like enough, or damned little. No blame to her for that. Earlier, when he and Sully had brought in Ekstrom's body and reported to Cyrus, telling him all — almost all — that had happened, Cyrus had said he would take care of telling Mrs. Ekstrom. So she'd been told; that was all he knew.

Sofie served the coffee and pulled up another chair by the fire. Her eyes were a bit reddened, but her face was steady again, her voice matter of fact. "Does Mr. Trapp move his cattle back now?"

"Soon as the weather breaks a little, I reckon. He'll want to pull 'em out of the Breaks before snow flies, and that'll be soon enough." Bowie sipped his coffee, watching the fire. "How much he tell about what happened?"

"Only that Jan was killed in the fight with the men who stole the cattle."

That was the version he and Sully had cooked up; they had confided the truth to Cyrus, who'd

154

agreed that no good would be served by giving out the real story. The man was dead and the best he could leave his widow was one good memory. "I want to tell you he went out like a brave man." The words soured Bowie's mouth; he didn't look at her. "I guess there's no more to say."

"No," she said soberly. "There is no more. If it's the truth, Mr. Candler."

The devil! What made her say that? "Yes'm. It's the truth."

He met her eyes with the lie, and she nodded slowly. "That is something then, eh? I don't mean to say bad of him, now he's gone, but there is so much —" Her face was troubled; she looked away. "It was not good with us, this you know. But it was not all his fault."

"Well, that is strictly your affair."

As if she hadn't heard, she went on musingly: "I don't blame Jan. Not now, thinking how it all was. He was a hard man, but his life made him so. My pa and me, we were very poor. He — my father drank a lot. So we did not have much money. Jan was our neighbor. He offered to help us because — because he liked me. I did not want his help, but when Pa took sick toward the end, there was the doctor to pay, no food in the house . . . I took his help then. And Pa left debts which must be paid. If I married Jan, he would pay them all. And he did. It seemed the right thing — then."

"I reckon it was."

"Do you think so? I do not know. Jan was not so hard a man then — gruff, you would say? — but not mean. This came when he lost the crops two years in a row. It was a good farm and he worked many years to make it so — and then, nothing there was but to sell out."

Bowie settled his head back, narrowing his eyes against the ribboning firelight. You never knew all of what was in anyone, he thought tiredly, till something happened to bring it out. Even then you were never sure. You kept stumbling on unexpected pockets in people you thought you knew. Take Sully. He wouldn't have suspected the streak of pure hardness Sully had shown after they'd taken Antrim's gang. Or take himself. Been years since he'd given a damn about much of anything. These weeks at Chainlink had shown him he could still care, by God, and that was something to know. Sofie. Her baby. Cyrus Trapp. Sully. They were all part of it, one way or another.

It felt good to pay off a debt too. Like Sully, he felt deep gratitude to Cyrus for taking him in, then for some kindred assurance that Cyrus had conveyed to him when they'd spoken together. Bigger things than they'd seemed. Odd that they'd both squared their debts to Cyrus with a lie: telling him that two of the cow thieves had escaped and omitting mention of Brady's and Joe-Bob's part. Would it be for the best? They could only hope.

He was half dozing. Sofie's voice pulled him

gently awake. "You are pretty tired, eh?"

"Been that kind of a job. Better get to my bunk before I get carried there." He stood up and so did Sofie; they looked at each other. He felt tentative and unsure. "You still plan on leaving here?"

"I cannot decide yet what I do, but I know I must work and earn my way. Mr. Trapp says I should stay the winter anyway."

"Maybe you should."

"I think so. I will help Mrs. Trapp with the household, whatever I can do. They are kind people here. You are kind."

Bowie's glance moved to the empty crib. "I was sorry to hear about your — about Eric."

"It is hard to think about yet. But this will pass. I think it was God's will — I do not know, but it's easier to think so. You tried to help, Mr. Candler. This I never forget."

"Well, you don't need to think about that."

"I never forget."

Bowie picked up his slicker and shrugged into it, feeling her eyes all the while. As he moved toward the door, she said: "Maybe you come again to talk? I like this if you would."

"Sure." He cleared his throat. "That would be fine."

It was a miserable Sunday afternoon and the crew didn't mind spending the day loafing around the bunkhouse, playing cards, mending clothes and gear, or dozing in their bunks. Faye

Nevers stood by the single small window that fronted on the yard, staring moodily out at the desolate weather. He felt restless — the sound of Barney's tinny harmonica irritated him; so did the mutters of the cardplayers and the deep snoring of Candler and Sully Calder in their bunks, sleeping off a sleepless night and the ordeal of their long stand at Yellow Pass.

Always alert to the politics of his position and Chainlink matters in general, the foreman had lately found more than enough to think about. Mostly he worried about Cyrus's deteriorating condition. Two days ago, after Cyrus had taken Ekstrom out to Yellow Pass to join Candler and Sully on watch (telling Nevers that he was taking Ekstrom to a line camp duty), he'd suffered an attack of head pains so severe that only a double dose of opiates had numbed it. Yesterday he'd been lurching about acting cockeyed and drunk, bumping into furniture, his speech slurring, giving contradictory orders and forgetting things he'd said only seconds before.

Cyrus was on his last legs; his days were running fewer. When they'd run out, what would Faye Nevers's prospects be? He hadn't an inkling of the contents of the will that was filed with Cyrus's attorney in Saltville. More than likely Cyrus, aware that he couldn't safely entrust his affairs to Brady's improvident hands, had made other provisions. By, say, leaving a controlling interest in Chainlink to Adah, with a stipulation that Nevers be retained as foreman.

That would be the sensible thing to do. But Jesus, how could he be sure? He couldn't go to Cyrus with a flat-out query; he'd learned long ago that Cyrus tolerated no prying in his personal business.

Looking out the window, Nevers stiffened to attention. That was Adah leaving the main house, wearing a riding habit. She hadn't gone for a ride more than twice since coming to Chainlink. Why choose a day like this for it? She was coming toward the bunkhouse. Guessing her purpose, Nevers made a quick decision.

When her knock came at the door, he lounged over to open it.

"Hello," she said. "Would you please have a man saddle a horse for me?"

"Sure thing. But it's a sorry day even for ducks."

"I am riding, nevertheless."

"All right," he said carelessly. "I'll saddle the horse myself." Ignoring the curious glances of the crew, he went to his bunk and pulled on his own slicker, then asked Hilo, smallest man on the crew, for the borrow of his. Hilo said sure. Nevers carried it to the doorway, saying, "You better wear this, Mrs. Trapp. You'll get pretty wet otherwise."

"Very well."

He held the bulky wrap while she slipped into it, then walked beside her as they crossed to the stable. Cold moisture had already stung her clear-cream skin with fresh color, and he had never seen a woman look so damned beautiful. "I'll ride with you if you've no objection," he said idly. "I mean if you plan on going far. Looks like the weather might get worse."

"If you like, Mr. Nevers."

He didn't ask questions; he could feel the tightness in her, reflected in her set lips and stiff tilt of head. A clash with her husband? Wouldn't be any wonder. This morning, the drugs worn off, Cyrus had been cranky and sharp, proddy as an old bull. Might be a fair day for a ride after all, Nevers thought speculatively.

They rode east from headquarters.

She held the sidesaddle well, but there was a hint of tension in her hard use of the bit. Nevers sensed that her usual placid temper was ruffled and any criticism would bring a sharp retort. The wind blew colder; sleet began to varnish the grass and earth with a tinselly jacket of ice. Grass blades crackled under the horses' hooves.

When Adah said, "We'll stop a minute. Please help me down," he merely nodded. Dismounting, he moved to her side and swung her to the ground. They were cut off from headquarters by a low hillock. Adah stepped away from him and stood gazing across the misty swells of dun-colored range eastward. Sleet slanted against the sides of their slickers; it prickled her face to a richer color.

"You want to go back now?" he asked.

"Not yet."

"What do you want, Mrs. Trapp?"

His dry and sardonic question, half amused, half impatient, brought her around facing him. Her eyes looked dark and driven; he felt a twist of heat rise in his belly. He couldn't read anything in her expression except a trace of fear. But fear of him or of herself? he wondered. Knowing that the growing, feverish attraction between them would never come to a head unless he forced it.

"I suggest that you mind your place. If I told my husband that you used such a tone to me, he'd horsewhip you off the ranch."

Nevers's patience thinned away. "But you won't tell him. That's the whole thing. Here —"

He took a step and enclosed her waist with one arm, his other hand roughly clamping her chin and twisting her face up. He kissed her for a long time and felt no fight in the heated bow of her body. Then he let go; she stepped backward, fisting both hands around the crop, but didn't raise it.

"You don't leave a person anything, do you?" she whispered.

"Not my fault if you lie to yourself about yourself."

"I didn't lie —" Her face was agonized, not angry; it resembled a crumpled petal. "But oh, God, it's wrong, so wrong. We're such different people. Why — tell me why!"

She was trembling all over as he took her in his arms, holding her tightly.

"I don't know why," he said gently. "But it's

161

not wrong. You don't believe that either."

"I don't know — it's all strange. Once, a long time ago it seems, my world was ordered and sensible. All of it was. Now —"

"No need to think on it." Nevers tightened his arms, smiling above her head. "I'll do all of that for both of us."

There was plenty to think about, by God. He felt a heady sense of power that made him want to laugh aloud.

CHAPTER ELEVEN

Two weeks went by before the season's first big snow hit the high country. Cyrus stood on the little stoop outside the entrance to his office and watched it come. The sky over the northern Elks was boiling with big smoky clouds roiled and driven by sliding, battering currents of wind. Some weather for sure. Real snow this time. There had been a few dismal flurries last week before the land had settled down to a silent frozen waiting. Now true winter was rushing in.

His last winter. The thought was a mere dull reflex, about all he could summon up these days. Cyrus wondered if he would live out this winter's end; he hoped not. Not if the steady failing of his strength and senses continued to the last. Even leaving his desk to come outside was a slow, labored ordeal.

He leaned a weary hand on the door frame, feeling sick and drained in every fiber of his being. His appetite had gone twelve days ago; his weight was melting away day by day; he could take a fistful of slack flesh on any part of his torso. In an incredibly compressed time his massive frame had withered to that of a huge-boned scarecrow, all the ravages of an advanced age he'd never see crushing down on him, blurring his eyes to horny film for long periods, riddling his memory with blank spots that would have broken another man to weeping frustration.

The pains were no more intense. They'd already ripped his brain and body with their exquisite worst; they merely came and went more frequently. Lately pain had come to seem like a perverse comrade. He now awaited the coming of each onslaught with a kind of fierce resigned pride; he could sit in stony endurance through interludes of agony that a month before would have reduced him to groaning fits. Always now he met it face on, grinding his will against it with an insensate fury until, gasping with a sense of bloodied triumph, he could let himself surrender to the double hypodermic that would bring a sodden twilight of unfeeling half-death where a man slid strangely back and forth on oblivion's edge. . . .

Christ, what a way to go.

Unless nature balanced its merciless toll with the final mercy before too damned long, he knew what he would do. God damned if he'd spend his last months as a helpless, bedridden wreck, unable to manage his simplest functions, babied by gruels and warming pans to a slobbering, mindless exit out of life. No, by God. A man deserved the dignity of final choice: his own way out.

Cyrus tipped his tired gaze down past the foothills to the old wagon road that crooked up from the terraced plains southwest, the road to Saltville. Man on horseback coming. A man

164

alone, pushing a brisk pace on the ice-rutted road. Not a grubline bum, Cyrus thought; this fellow rode like a man with a mission. Whoever it was, he had good reason to complete it and be on his way with that hellsmear of a storm threatening to break before the day was out.

While he was slowly forming these thoughts, the rider reached the haysheds at the east edge of the corrals and swung his mount up toward the house yard. Damned if it wasn't Beamis. Old Sam himself. He hadn't seen the old rawhide bastard in six months. Something warmed and thawed in Cyrus's chest; his mouth jerked in a grin. He always felt good on seeing Sam again, and never more than now. Not very many men in this country went back as far as he and Sam did, to its raw pioneer roots.

Sheriff Beamis raised a thick arm in greeting as he halted at the rail that sided the veranda. Swinging heavily to the ground, he tied his horse and tramped over to the side entrance. Cyrus noted the veiled shock in Beamis's eyes under the tufted brows as he extended a burly hand; Sam was finding it hard to believe this was the same Cyrus Trapp he'd known for three and a half decades.

"Hello, you goddam old catamount."

"How you doing, Cyrus?"

Beamis's lips twisted faintly as if with instant regret at the inference in a casual greeting. He was a squat buffalo of a man in his late fifties, with a face like a sleepy bulldog's and a full head of stiff gray-shot black hair.

"Pretty obvious, ain't it?" Cyrus said dryly. "Well, let's don't stand out here cooling our butts. Come inside." They stepped into the small cluttered office; Cyrus motioned his visitor to a chair. "What brings you over this way on such a day?"

Beamis unbuttoned his mackinaw and settled into the chair. "Oh, some business. Nothing important. While I was here, thought I'd drop by for a chat."

Cyrus backed to his swivel chair and, gripping its arms and clenching his teeth, carefully lowered himself into it. He studied Beamis's impassive face and smiled sardonically. "Sure as hell you did. With a sight of mean weather ready to hit every foot of road between here and Saltville. You'll be riding out a blizzard before you reach home, Sam."

Beamis grunted, crossing his thick legs. "Well, there's just no easy way to say it. Heard talk you was doing poorly of late, so debated some whether you should be told right away. Don't seem no odds in putting it off."

"Christ, Sam, will you kindly not bandy words with me? We known each other too long."

"Yeah," Beamis said bleakly. "To cut it brief, then. Few days ago a couple hardcases named Blue Searls and Arch Quade tried for the bank up at Craigie. Heard about a big safe full of cattle-sale money and decided they wanted it. They didn't make it, but killed young Seth Win-

166

ters, the cashier, after he went for a hideout gun. They panicked and run, but Searls had this bum leg that slowed 'em down. My deputy at Craigie, Jim Wetherall, captured 'em both."

"Good for him." Cyrus's brows lifted. "Searls and Quade, huh? I know the names. Both of 'em were sidekicks of Red Antrim's. They'd be the two that got away when a pair of my crew busted Antrim's gang back in the Breaks two weeks ago. Hell, I sent you word about it."

"I got your word. Thing is, this blue-ribbon pair claim they didn't get away from your men. Claimed, in fact, that they got turned loose by 'em."

Cyrus's eyes slitted down; he heaved painfully forward in the chair. "That sounds fine. Suppose you tell me just what the hell it means."

"I'm coming to it. Quade'll hang for killing Winters and he knows it. Likely on account he's got nothing to lose, he opened up about all the little sidelines Antrim had cooking, from whiskey-peddling to the Utes to high-grading your cows. Out of pure spite, I'd say, he implicated half a dozen gentlemen, solid citizens all, who'd been secretly involved in various shady deals with Antrim one time or another. Then Searls got talking; he backed up everything Quade said. I been checking back on all they told us. So far they ain't lied."

"What the hell's that got to do with what you said about my men?"

"Easy there. You don't need to fret about your

men. Seems they covered up purely on your account."

"Sam, make sense, Goddammit!"

Beamis shifted uncomfortably. "Quade and Searls both claim there was two others in with Antrim on high-grading that stuff of yours. Your sons. Brady and Joe-Bob."

Cyrus said nothing. Just looked at him unblinkingly.

Beamis talked on quietly. A gambling debt, Quade had said. Lucky Jack Hackett held Brady's notes for over a thousand dollars. Brady had agreed to sign a rigged bill of lading for Antrim's buyer; his share would redeem his IOUs from Hackett. Beamis had gone to Lucky Jack and asked him about the notes.

"And?" Cyrus said hoarsely.

"Had to lean on him some before he showed me the IOUs. Said he'd threatened Brady with going to you unless he paid up. Those two men of yours wouldn't be around, would they?"

Cyrus stared at the floor, slowly rubbing his temple. His arm felt numb and heavy; a ragged pulse beat in each fingertip. Patiently Beamis repeated the question.

"What? Oh, Candler and Sully?" Cyrus shook his head heavily. "They — they're out riding line. They should be in before long."

"They'll know what the truth is. You can get it out of 'em; I likely couldn't." The sheriff rose and walked to the window, peering out. "Gonna be a helldimmer, that storm. I better be getting

168

back home." He walked to the door and paused, hand on the latch. "Cyrus, we been friends a long time. It's your sons, your cattle, we been talking about. I'll leave it to you what's to be done. You can prefer charges or not. Take your time; think on it. Send me word what you decide." Another pause. "One thing. The story can't be hushed up. Quade will talk at his trial. Then it'll be public record."

Cyrus scrubbed a hand over his face. He nodded once, up and down.

Beamis said gently then, "I'm sorry to see you like this, Cyrus."

"I'm sorry you had to." Cyrus lifted his head with an effort. "Sam. Much obliged."

"Sure," Beamis said glumly. "Take care. I'll see you again."

"Wouldn't count on that this side of hell."

When the sheriff had gone, Cyrus sat unmoving for a long time. A red slow fury began to sizzle at the back of his brain. Twitches of raw and violent impulse shook him; he damped each one down. But the effort to stay calm started him shaking uncontrollably. Calm — Christ. How could he be calm!

Brady — Brady, God damn you.

He didn't have to question Candler or Sully. He knew the answer already, knew it as surely as he did the core of Brady's miserable-pup soul. His sons. God. The only flesh and blood of his own he could leave in this world. His sons. The words had a naked echoing mockery. Like cold laughter, savage and shattering. Blood thickening in his head brought the relentless knife of his pain, that familiar comrade of fierce agony and heavy sweats, pressing in. *Come on, you bastard, come on.* He needed something to fight. Something to contain the waiting edge of his rage until Brady and Joe-Bob returned from Saltville, where they had gone to throw a spree.

We're gonna get drunk, Brady had arrogantly told him before slamming out of the house, he letting them go because, weakened and dull, he no longer gave a damn.

Had thought he didn't.

It was graying toward dusk, the snow beating down thick and fast, as Brady and Joe-Bob came off the Saltville road into Chainlink headquarters. The storm had caught them halfway home and by now both were reasonably sobered. They angled past the cookshack. Lights squared the windows; the crew was at supper. They rode on to the stable and dismounted unsteadily.

The cookshack door scraping open pulled Brady's watery glance; someone came out. Brady couldn't identify his dark figure through the torrent of swirling flakes, but he was heading diagonally across the yard toward the old house Cyrus had turned over to the Ekstroms. That would be Bowie Candler — a frequent caller these days on the widow Ekstrom. Brady tasted hatred like a vicious bile; just thinking of Candler could do it for him.

He dragged open the stable doors. Joe-Bob could hardly stand; he was gulping wretchedly as they led the horses inside. Brady lighted a bull's-eye lantern and hung it on a post. His head was pounding; his savage mood deepened. He was in no damn mood to face Cyrus, though he hadn't caught hell from the old man in some time. When he'd unsaddled the horses and turned them into the stalls, he pawed through the hay in a vacant stall till he located a half-empty bottle he'd cached there several days ago. Uncorking it, he took a long swig and held the bottle out to Joe-Bob, who was crouching in the clay runway, head between his knees.

"Better have one, kid. It'll put some hair in your gullet."

Joe-Bob shook his head without raising it. "I — I'm gonna be sick, Brady."

"Go ahead. Fighting nature ain't no odds."

Joe-Bob threw up, dry-retching afterward for a half minute. When he got to his feet, he was pale and shaking. "Gonna go up to the house — go to bed."

"You do that. I got some thinkin' and drinkin' to do first. I'll be along. Go on."

Joe-Bob stumbled out; Brady hauled the doors shut. Tramping over to the empty stall, he settled himself in the hay and took another long pull from the bottle. Getting slowly drunk again put an edge on his blackly bitter thoughts. He'd dreaded facing Lucky Jack Hackett today, but had known he couldn't put it off much longer.

171

Mustering cold courage, he'd told Hackett that he'd be unable to pay what he owed him now or very soon. Had all but gone on his knees to the son of a bitch. Lucky Jack had been unsympathetic. You got one more week, he'd said, and then I pay a call on your old man.

Well, that tore it sure. Cyrus's wrath would be monumental, but even that might not be the worst of it. Overshadowing everything was the threat that Candler and Sully could divulge his collaboration with Antrim any time they had a mind to. Brady remembered Sully's warning: *You slip just once for that old man to see. . . .*

If he got the old man upset and they learned of it, what then?

There was still the bleak option he'd discarded before. Throw himself on Cyrus's mercy and hope. Brady hadn't seriously considered that it would do any good, but he'd come close to it a couple times. Trouble was, anything he started to tell his father always came out as sass. He couldn't help it; something in the old man's manner scraped him raw every time he tried talking to him. Far back as he could remember, his father had loomed across his world like a frowning, bearded titan. Prodding him always to measure up, savagely castigating him when he couldn't. How in hell could anyone measure up to Cyrus Trapp's standards?

True, the old man had softened in recent years. Enough to dumfound Brady, who'd modeled all his precepts on the harsh and roughshod

Cyrus of his boyhood. And lately, watching the titan of memory wasting away before his eyes, he'd realized that the old Cyrus was no more; only a failing, indifferent husk remained. Was there a shred of hope in that fact? Sinking toward his end, Cyrus might be willing to call quits to every old score — and forgive. Yeah — he might just be approachable as hell now. If, Brady thought, he could screw down his temper and blunt ancient resentments with a few more drinks, he'd be mellow enough to beard the old bastard in a reasonable tone.

His fast fiery pulls at the bottle had nearly drained it, warming his confidence and giving a slushy twist to his thoughts. He wondered how Candler was doing with the widow Ekstrom. God damn! Imagine that scruffy pilgrim stepping in and taking over slick as pie. Lucky bastard. A lush piece like her could warm up a lot of winter nights. That smooth leggy walk put you in mind of wind curving a young pine. And man, what a set of jugs on her.

He struggled unsteadily to his feet. He felt sickish, his head swimming, and had to grab at the stall partition for support.

In the same instant one of the double doors burst open and cold air lashed him. A moment later Joe-Bob, propelled by a powerful shove, plunged through the open doors and fell in a headlong sprawl on the runway. After him came Cyrus; he jammed the door shut behind them.

Brady gaped at him. Cyrus's face looked

swollen with rage; he loomed in the lantern light, his shadow flung huge and formless on the wall. His fists were closing and unclosing.

"Pa — ?"

Cyrus came tramping up to Brady. Without a word, he swung his big palm. The blow smacked Brady's jaw like a club, tearing loose his hold on the partition. He landed in the runway on his hip and shoulder, rolled over once, and stopped on his back. He simply lay as he'd fallen, paralyzed with whiskey and shock. Reaching down, Cyrus fisted a handful of Brady's mackinaw, dragged him to his feet, and slammed him against the support post.

"We'll hear some truth from you for a change," Cyrus said hoarsely. "I heard plenty already. First from Beamis, then your simple pup of a brother. But it's really you, boy. You're the one."

His knotted fist was doubled up into Brady's throat, almost crushing off his wind. Brady clamped his hand around his father's wrist, but he couldn't summon the strength to break the savage grip. Blind fury was feeding Cyrus's ravaged body with a strength beyond itself.

"Your partners got caught. Searls and Quade —" Cyrus jerked Brady forward and back, crashing his head on the post. "They told Beamis everything. Now —" Again Brady's head slammed against the post. "You tell your old pa all about it!"

"Leggo, Pa," Brady choked. "*Jeezus* —"

"Just as soon as you talk. Then I let go. Then I

mean to kick the living shit out of you, you thieving bastard!"

Joe-Bob was on his hands and knees, stupefied with terror, lank hair falling in his eyes. Scrambling to his feet now, he lunged at his father, seizing his arm. "Don't, Pa. Don't go hurting Brady —"

He nearly succeeded in wrestling Cyrus away, and then Cyrus roared "God damn!" and half-pivoted, lashing back with his free hand. It caught Joe-Bob flush on the temple and sent him stumbling backward. Momentarily free of Cyrus's pressing weight, Brady flung himself sideways, breaking Cyrus's hold. Stumbling wildly away, he was groggy but cold-headed now, tasting brassy fear.

Cyrus started after him, a great vein pulsing in his neck.

"Don't, don't do it, Pa," Brady wheezed. "Don't you lay a hand on me again, by God!"

"You gonna do nothing," Cyrus whispered, "except get booted clear off Chainlink. You won't be able to walk away when I'm done with you —"

A mad light quivered in his eyes. God, he's gone out of his head, he's going to kill me! The single thought flashed through Brady's mind with chill clarity before Cyrus's fist caught him full in the face.

Brady backpedaled, tripped, and fell into a stall. He shook his head, blood drops spraying from his pulped nose, then surged to his feet, fingers clawing for support. They closed on a pitch-fork rammed in some loose hay; he yanked it free.

He tried to lunge out of the stall, but Cyrus, coming on bear-big and red-eyed, had blocked him off. Cornered, Brady screeched, *"Pa, don't!"* And swung the pitchfork up and forward in a desperate unthinking reflex. The tines flashed wickedly, momentarily, before Cyrus's deep-flung shadow dulled them as he came bulling straight on. Unthinkingly Brady braced his weight to meet the charge —

Cyrus's body ran onto the twin prongs with the full force of his rush. He staggered back, clutching at his belly. Red wetness crawled over his clenched fingers. He sighed, a soft explosive "Ah!" and turned slowly on his heel and walked out of the stall.

Brady dropped the pitchfork. Watched in sick dreading fascination as Cyrus halted in the runway. Then Cyrus's legs caved; he fell to his knees, his wet hands lifting to his head. He pressed them against his temples as if trying to squeeze out the intolerable agony that twisted his face.

His hands dropped; his body canted forward. He pitched on his face and was motionless.

Brady's legs moved; twists of hay crackled under his feet. Feeling nothing at all, he knelt by Cyrus. His arms felt weak as water. It took all his strength to heave his father's body over on its back.

176

Joe-Bob was whimpering, "Pa, Pa, Pa . . ."

"Shut up," Brady muttered.

"You killed him. You killed Pa."

"He killed himself. Shut your goddam mouth. I got to think."

Brady rasped a palm over his face, trying to scour feeling back into his numb flesh. God, you done it now, haven't you? You really done it. Goddam those two oozing wounds. They weren't deep enough to kill. That thing eating in Cyrus's head had really killed him; he might have gone any time. But no question that the shock of being double-stabbed in the guts had triggered his premature end. And not a way under the sun you could cover up the fact.

No. That somebody had stabbed Cyrus was unarguable. You couldn't cover that. But why did it have to be him? Brady's mind began racing with hot calculation. Tula, he knew, had left Chainlink yesterday in order to visit some Indian friends halfway across the valley; she hadn't returned yet.

"Kid. Listen to me. When Pa collared you in the house, was there anyone else about?"

Joe-Bob's face glittered with tears; he gazed dumbly at his brother.

"Snap to, Goddammit! Did anyone else see it? Was Adah there?"

"Uh — I didn't see 'er. She mighta been in bed with one of them headaches. You know how she gets."

Yeah. Dead to the world when she had to sleep

off a headache. If so, it was unlikely she'd heard anything either.

"Brady, what we gonna do? What we gonna do now?"

"Well," Brady said softly, "we ain't gonna bawl over it."

Standing now, he tramped over to his brother. Roughly cupped his hand around Joe-Bob's chin, squeezing it between thumb and fingers. Joe-Bob winced; Brady shook him gently. "You're in this with me. Don't you forget it. No matter what anyone asks, you say what I'll tell you to say. Just that. We're gonna come out of this smelling like spring flowers."

Clean as a whistle, Brady thought. If it worked — his mind sprinted exultantly ahead to all that might be. If it worked.

CHAPTER TWELVE

"Then I mustanged in the Mogollon country," Bowie said. "That's catching wild horses. I caught and rough-broke plenty till my bones began to brittle up. Happens way before a man turns thirty."

"Long ago Mr. Trapp did so too," Sofie observed. "He told me."

Bowie smiled. "Yeah, only he worked for himself and saved his money. I worked for an outfit for wages and generally blowed what I earned in a few days. You know, drinking and things. Course a man learns. I finally laid by a good stake and throwed in with another fellow, Danny Spike, on a little freight line. Only there was a bigger outfit freighting the same route between Silver City and Redrock. When we cut rates, they didn't like it. Shot our mules and burned us out."

"*Himmel,* was there no law?"

"Law don't always shine for the little man. This top dog owned a lot more than we did, including a bought sheriff and judge. Danny and I busted up and drifted our own ways. What I heard of Dan later on, he got killed in a gambling scrape in Redrock."

Bowie fell silent in his chair, gazing at the crackling fire. Friends. He had buried a few. Others he hardly remembered. The faces came

179

and went over the years, jostling and merging in memory, and after a while most of them seemed the same. It was no different with the jobs. Bunkhouses you called home while you sweated or froze your ass for the fatcats who owned the ranches, the mines, the lumbering operations. Sometimes you tried striking on your own; he'd dredged up a few of those memories for Sofie tonight. Memories that seemed even bleaker in the telling than in the way they totaled to beat a man down over the years. But talking about them smacked of self-pity, which his fierce pride rejected. Hell, most men he'd worked with lived with their lot and bitched as a matter of course, rarely feeling sorry for themselves. The ones who did cracked apart without fanfare. Hanging themselves maybe, or whipping razors across their throats. It was too bad, but life had to go on. Like old Cyrus had said, long as you could keep the candle going was worth it.

Sofie gently broke the silence. "What do you think of now?"

"Nothing much."

"Oh *ja,* Bowie. You think a lot." She laughed. "You hardly talk at all, you think sad things so much. Your face, I can tell. I like to sit and wonder what does he think of."

"Man like that can be pretty tiresome."

"No. No, not to talk is all right when that is a man's way. But you talk a lot tonight, more than you have before. This I like too, but I don't like to think you're sad."

180

Bowie felt a faint embarrassment. He could tell her that sadness as she meant it wasn't a part of it any longer. But how to say such a thing? To say it all, he'd have to laboriously explain how it seemed that every time a man got something going for him, it would sour out. That after a time he sickened of even trying. That he blamed nothing and nobody for it, but that didn't change how the bill always totted up. That these two weeks of evenings by her fireplace had left him with something altogether different. That watching Sofie and listening to her quick lilt of words and laughter tickled up a good warmth that made him lighthearted (or lightheaded, he wasn't sure which) in a way he'd never known.

Hell, he couldn't tell her all that; he wouldn't know how to begin. Or how to get out a lot more that kept crowding to his mind and became harder to crowd out. Sofie had married a failure of a man; she deserved better next time around. This was the sadness, sharp and regretful, that coupled with the goodness of these times in her company. He couldn't take more from her than a string of gentle firelit evenings allowed when all he could give in return was a mass of failings. What else could he lay claim to?

"I better be turning in," he said, getting to his feet. "Have to look to my horse too."

"*Ja*, the horse. You always look to him."

"Well, I worry he'll take the green heaves from grain-feeding sometime. You never know about a high-plains mustang."

181

"No wonder you worry, an animal so fine to look at. Has he a name?"

"Uh — Kicker. I call him Kicker."

Pulling on his mackinaw, he looked at her standing in the firelight. Straight and firm-bodied and very young-looking in an old calico dress. Her hair was done in a single thick braid twisted in a coronet atop her head; it caught the light like pale flame. It was getting harder to push away what he couldn't say and feared he might. Damn. Maybe he shouldn't have started these visits. But he knew he wasn't sorry. That he wouldn't stop them, either, unless or until she said the word.

"Good night, my good friend. Maybe I will pray you don't be sad any more."

Bowie colored a little. That was her straight-faced way of laughing at him, with a gentle warmth that made it stingless.

As he tramped across to the stables, the warmth stayed with him; it reached to his insides like a soft hand. The snow was pelting down so thickly that it veiled the ranch buildings to dark blurs; it had a fresh squeaky crunch under his boots. Coming to the stable doors, he reached for the swingbar and found it off the brackets; somebody must be inside.

He dragged one door open, stepped inside, and came to a dead halt. The dim light of a bull's-eye showed him a scene he couldn't believe.

Brady waved his pistol slightly, motioning

with it. "All the way in, pilgrim. Then shut the door."

Bowie slowly obeyed. Then he took the scene in wholly, feeling chilled to his guts. Brady facing him spraddle-legged, gun pointed. Joe-Bob crouching on his heels, looking furtive and miserable. Cyrus stretched on his back in the runway, his face waxen and still.

"What's happened here?"

"See for yourself."

Brady moved aside and Bowie tramped past him and bent down by Cyrus. His mouth was partly open, his eyes sightless. Touching his face, Bowie found the flesh already cold. He saw sticky darkness on Cyrus's coat and started his hand toward it.

"That's enough," Brady said softly. "You got the idea."

Tight-throated, Bowie shook his head. "No, I don't get it. You — *you?*"

"It was an accident. Kind of your doing too, ridgerunner. How you like that?"

Bowie stood up now, watching Brady's face. It held a heavy mockery, the jaws grooved with tension. Blood crusted his nose.

"You should of shot them two yahoos you turned loose, boy," Brady said. "Seems they got caught and spilled everything to Beamis. All about me and Joe-Bob. So the old man came r'aring after me. Way it happened, he just r'ared hisself to death. Might of happened different if you'd been honest with him first place."

"You son of a bitch."

"Yeah, but I'm gonna be the live one." Brady shifted his feet, grinning. "Like I say, it was an accident. We won't pretend it was nothing else. Only you gonna be the one that pushed the old bastard over the edge." He slapped a bottle that bulged the pocket of his coat, its neck protruding. "You asked what happened here. All right, I tell you, pilgrim. The old man run out of that stuff he's been injecting in him to kill his goddam pains. He had to fall back on booze. You want to know what booze did to my old man? Turned him crazy. As much like to attack friend as foe." Brady jerked out a flat chuckle. "Well sir, he went clean out of his head, that's what. Cornered you down here and they wasn't much you could do but defend yourself. With that."

He pointed at a pitchfork on the floor. Its tines, Bowie saw, were stained at the tips as though something wetly dark had frozen on them.

"Too goddam bad about that," Brady went on. "I mean, hell, Adah knows how Cyrus got when he had some redeye in him. So does Nevers. Likewise Tula. Too bad you didn't know, pilgrim, 'cause see, you'd have a good self-defense plea. Only you didn't know. After you killed him, you panicked and went kiting off in the storm, nobody knows where. When the storm lets up, your tracks'll be long gone. Longer than anybody's gonna realize, boy. That is, till they turn up your body come spring."

Bowie was getting the picture. Not all of it. But enough to turn a man's guts. "Who you think's going to believe all that?"

Brady laughed. "It don't make such bad sense, pilgrim. Why you figure we been waiting here for you near an hour? Hell, everyone knows you been cozying your ass over at the widow Ekstrom's ever' night around this time. Ain't no secret either you always have a last look at that buckskin before you turn in."

"That's what brought me here," Bowie said softly. "What you suppose brought your pa?"

"Why, horseshit, man, who knows why somebody who goes off his head from a lick of booze does anything he does when he's got some in him?"

Bowie shook his head. "It won't work. It's got too big a smell about it."

"Brady," Joe-Bob said shakily, coming up off his haunches, "you know, he's right. I mean, we run into Sam Beamis on the road and he give us a godawful funny look. He knows about us and Antrim, he —"

"He told the old man, sure. But he didn't arrest us directly he clapped eyes on us, why not? I'll tell you why, lunkhead. 'Cause the old man told Beamis he wasn't pressing charges. If that was the old man's last word to him, Beamis ain't gonna stir up the kettle on't now, not the kind of friends they was."

"But Jeez, Brady, he's gonna figure we musta

185

tangled with the old man soon's we got home —"

"It don't make no goddam difference what he thinks," Brady snapped. "He's gotta have proof. Told you, we're gonna set it up to look like pilgrim here done it, and we're gonna tell it that way. Unless Beamis can prove otherwise, he's gotta accept our story."

"But Jeez, he'll *know* — *!*"

"Shut up!" Brady half shouted, tense muscles ridging his face. Sweat glistened on his cheekbones. "It'll work like I said if you just keep your goddam head!" His voice quieted. "I'll do the talking when the time comes, but you got to back me all the way. One wrong word and you'll kick over the bucket. Keep the story straight and we'll have everything. Every damn thing. . . ."

As he talked, Brady tramped over to his father's body, pulled the bottle from his pocket, drew the cork with his teeth, and poured a little of the remaining liquor into Cyrus's mouth. The rest he spilled on Cyrus's shirt where his coat fell open. He straightened with a grunt, ramming the bottle back in his pocket.

"All right, pilgrim. Fling your hull on that buckskin. Then saddle that bay of mine."

"You go to hell," Bowie said quietly.

Brady tipped his gun up. "You want it right here?"

"That won't do your story a lot of good, will it?"

With a savage curse, Brady took two long steps and swung his pistol, slashing the barrel across

Bowie's temple. He grabbed at his head as he fell to his hands and knees, pinwheels of pain rocking his skull. Dimly he heard Brady say, "Get his saddle on, kid. Hurry it up."

When the two horses were readied, Brady bent and grabbed Bowie roughly by the shoulder. "On your feet, damn you. Get up on that nag unless you want more of the same."

Bowie staggered against the buckskin's flank as Joe-Bob held the animal steady. For a moment he held to the pommel, sickly mustering his strength, and then he swung up. Brady stepped into his saddle, saying, "It's gonna work for us, kid. You do like I said. Get up to the house and clean the old man's supply of drugs out of his desk. Don't miss nothing. Here, take this bottle — leave it in his office. Then get back here and wait for me. Got that?"

Joe-Bob nodded dumbly.

"Open them doors for us. Pilgrim, you ride out ahead of me. I'll tell you where to go."

They skirted wide of the bunkhouse, dark and silent now in the skirling snow which almost hid it from view. The crew was all abed, Bowie thought, setting his teeth against the battering ache of his head. But they wouldn't be abed too long; he could picture how it would go. Brady excitedly arousing them with the news: Cyrus dead in the stable and he'd seen Bowie taking flight. Or would Brady handle it another way? The details didn't matter. Soon the increasing wind would sweep all the tracks smooth, making

Brady's story unshakable. As he'd said, it might smell to high heaven some ways; but who could disprove it?

At Brady's order, Bowie pointed the buckskin toward the north peaks. He couldn't make out much in the shroud of blowing snow, but Brady had an unerring eye for the few dimly seen landmarks; he knew where he was going and his cursing commands kept Bowie headed on what seemed like a straight course.

Snowflakes whipped Bowie's face in deepening gusts; his eyes stung and watered. He clamped his hat low and hunched his head into his turned-up collar. The snow still mantled the frozen ground thinly, letting the horses move at a steady pace. But in a few hours, Bowie knew, it would be drifted a foot or more deep. The full cold certainty of his predicament was settling into his marrow. Wherever Brady chose to dispose of him, his snow-covered corpse wouldn't be found till spring.

Chainlink's rolling north range extended far into the foothills country. Northwest were the Breaks; northeasterly, the land climbed toward the high passes through which Bowie had come south weeks ago. He guessed they were moving in that general direction, which made sense enough if he were clearing out in panic, as Brady's version would have it. But how far did Brady intend taking him? Probably not too far, with the storm threatening to develop into a lot worse.

About the time he could feel the ground tending to rise, Bowie made out a black broken spine of ridges against the lighter sky ahead of them. Almost before he realized it they were moving sharply upward through stunted pines; they were on an age-old trail that the Indians had probably used. Wind whistled through the pine tops, which somewhat broke the storm's force. Occasionally he glanced back at Brady's dark muffled form. He couldn't see the pistol, but Brady would have it close to hand.

His only chance lay in making a break for it, but so far there'd been no possibility of bringing it off. Brady kept close on his heels, never falling more than three yards behind. Nor was he likely to find an opportunity unless the storm increased in fury, enough to cover his break beyond the distance he'd gain on the steep gamble that he could catch Brady briefly off guard.

Suddenly they came out of the trees, and then they were climbing straight upward across black spurs of shale outcrop; the horses' hooves skidded slickly here and there. Here in the high open the wind shrieked down off the heights, buffeting men and mounts with icy fists. Bowie felt his horse shudder and snort as they came unexpectedly against a sheer rock wall, or what felt like one.

"To your right!" Brady yelled. "Push on right — there's a trail."

Not very goddam much of a trail. It was

treacherously narrow, bending out of sight where the wall curved away. Bowie's spine crawled as he edged the buckskin along it, feeling out every step on the snow-frosted rock. On one side the wall soared almost straight upward; on the other, so far as he could tell, the trail lipped off in a snow-swirling gulf. A gorge that was deep but pretty narrow, he could make out the opposite rim.

Jesus! He felt a chill certainty before Brady spoke.

"Stop where you are, pilgrim."

Bowie halted, looking back over his shoulder. He didn't dare to make any other move on this slender ribbon of ledge. Brady hadn't advanced a step onto the ledge trail. He sat his horse waiting, and now he cocked his gun. The metal *snack-snack* was crisp and specific.

"You run your last ridge, boy. End of the trail."

"You think I'll just hop off here for your convenience, that it?"

They were half-shouting; the wind tore their words away.

"That or get shot off. Your choice!"

"Horse and me'll get found come spring, Brady. Think about it!"

"You was pushing hard when you lit out. You don't know the country good, you took a bad trail, you slipped here and went over. Both of you. That's how it'll look."

"With a bullet in me?" Bowie jeered. "There

might be enough left of me to show a bullet hole. How'll you explain that? Because you'll sure-hell have to put one in me, Junior. Go ahead."

Deliberately he heeled the buckskin forward along the ledge trail. A few more yards and he would pass out of Brady's sight, and now he braced for the worst.

Brady fired, but not at him. The shot creased the buckskin. He squealed and surged crazily against the wall; rock gouged Bowie's leg. Brady shot again as Bowie kicked out of his stirrups and scrambled sideways, trying to leave the saddle. The buckskin was fiddlefooting in pain and terror, and then he bolted. Instantly his hooves skidded; his sloughing weight went out of control and over the edge of the rimrock.

Bowie dropped free of the falling horse, hitting the ledge in a loose horsebreaker's roll. Landing on his back, he felt one leg slip over the rim; he tried to twist onto his belly and claw for a hold, but too late. His hand closed on wet snow and slick rock, and then his whole body went over.

He was plunging down a rough slant, body straight and head up, but there was nothing to hold onto. Only loose snow and rotted shale that broke and clattered downward under his scrambling hands. In the same instant that his feet slid off into nothing, his fingers closed on a projecting nub of rock. For a moment it stopped his fall, but it was too slick and shallow for him to gain purchase. Abruptly his hands slipped off.

He dropped several yards in a free fall, then

struck a lower slant of the gorge wall with a force that battered him numb, body and senses. Afterward he bounced and scraped downward on a steepening pitch, flinty points ripping at his clothing and flesh. Suddenly this slant too ended. A moment of cold space and rushing darkness. Then he hit bottom with an impact he hardly felt. Lit on his feet, but his buckling legs flailed away his footing and his body slammed on frozen earth. A smashing blow on the head. Then the world spun away from his last flicker of sensibility.

CHAPTER THIRTEEN

Sully Calder lay awake in his bunk, watching the dim square of window on the south wall. When it began to turn light, he would make his move. Not before. Around him the vague snores and grunts of sleeping men made a rude blending above the seething whisper of snow against the outer walls. Funny how men slept. Some as silent as death; others grumping and tossing; some with sodden snorings like buzzsaws cutting wet wood. He'd never particularly noticed such differences before, but tonight, his nerves alert and waiting, Sully had catalogued the sleeping habits of every man in the bunkhouse.

Just a manner of whiling away the time. That and thinking. But he'd pretty well worried every thought in his head to extinction. Only false dawn might offer some of the answers. All he'd need was sufficient dull light to track by. Luckily the wind appeared to be holding low so that, God willing, there'd be undrifted sign enough for him to follow.

Sully forced himself to relax and go over the whole thing again. Brady's account of what had happened hinged on coincidence that wasn't so wildly improbable in itself. It just might have occurred that way. What gave his story such a patently false ring to Sully's mind was knowing the people involved as he did.

193

Way Brady had told it, he and Joe-Bob had returned from Saltville and were approaching the stable, thinking it funny the doors were hanging open, when a rider had come lunging out of the building, spurring his horse wildly. Nothing but a dark shape in the storm, he was quickly swallowed by it. The brothers, hurrying into the stable, had found their father's body. The rest, if you wanted to believe Brady, was clear as spring water. Hell, a blind man could figure how it had gone. Cyrus had found Candler in the stable looking to his horse. Christ, who knew what reason the old man had for going down there? Likely no reason. He smelled hog-high of booze and it was no secret what effect liquor had on him. He must have attacked Candler, who'd defended himself with the pitchfork. Lightly stabbed in the guts, Cyrus had died then and there: the final shock to his system. Candler? He'd simply panicked and run out. He'd already followed Candler's tracks a short way, Brady added, but he was too far ahead to overtake in the night and storm. Natural enough to cut out like he did, figuring odds wouldn't favor anyone believing it had been an accident.

Natural for some men, Sully thought. But Bowie Candler getting that badly rattled? Sully's instant reaction had been one of flat disbelief, though he'd said nothing. Only after Brady had roused the crew and they were all in the stable, gazing at the body and listening to Brady's reconstruction of what must have happened, had

194

Sully put a casual question to Brady.

"You touch the body at all?"

"No," Brady growled. "Why should I?"

Sully pointed at an isolated patch of blood which had soaked into the clay two feet from Cyrus's body. "That looks like he fell on his belly. No other wound on him, is there?"

"Well, he must of turned over before he died. Or maybe Candler turned him over."

Sully nodded soberly. "Yeah. That'd be it, I guess."

But the unexpected question had caught Brady off balance. Something in the tight, defensive way he'd responded suggested a man who hadn't adjusted all sides of his story. If Faye Nevers thought anything was fishy, he'd masked his thoughts, merely listening to Brady and saying little. But that was like Faye. It was he who'd gone up to the house to break the news to Adah Trapp.

Anyway, Brady had gone on pointedly, it had to be Candler, didn't it? He was gone; so was his buckskin horse. And Nevers, returning from the house, had confirmed that the drugs Cyrus had kept in his desk were gone too — and he'd found an empty whiskey bottle. But a number of factors, as Sully sized them up, didn't jog into place at all.

If Cyrus had run low on pain killers, why hadn't he renewed his supply before now? And where had he gotten the booze? Tula had said that after Cyrus's drunken fit some weeks ago,

Mrs. Trapp had ordered her to throw out every drop of liquor in the house; Tula had done so. It was unbelievable that Cyrus, hardly a man to compound one near-tragic mistake, would conceal a bottle somewhere. Something else too: Sully had taken the opportunity to touch Cyrus's face, its flesh cold in death. If he'd been killed only minutes before Brady had rousted out the crew, how had the heat run out of his body so quickly?

He wouldn't be the only one puzzling over those questions, Sully reflected grimly. Trouble was, even if they did riddle the situation with suspicious overtones, mere unanswered questions couldn't discredit Brady's story. Only Bowie Candler could do that.

And where was Bowie?

That he'd ridden away on the buckskin seemed unarguable. Sully had checked the tracks leading to and from the stable — and that was something else. The prints left by the returning Trapp brothers were deeply blurred by the fast-falling snow, yet to a considerably lesser extent than the horse tracks leading out in the storm. But these, too, had already been blown into as if a far longer time had elapsed since they were made than Brady's telling would bear out.

The whole damn business had more holes in it than a wormy apple.

Most of all, Sully wondered what had really happened to Bowie. His concern for his friend was as keen as his shock of grief at Cyrus's death.

That had been expected; yet a man like Cyrus Trapp deserved at least the dignity of a decent end. Not an interpretation which said he'd been stabbed with a pitchfork while in the throes of a drunken rage. Thinking about it all, Sully felt a clean and feral anger that honed his determination sharper.

All right. Carry it a step farther. Had Brady arranged a deliberate frame-up against Bowie? Even considering Brady's hatred of him, that didn't seem likely. The situation as it stood smelled of a hasty improvising. Brady, give him credit, had brains enough to concoct a frame far more cunningly rigged than this leaky piece of business. The real circumstances of Cyrus's death remained unclear; all Sully could dredge up were uncertain guesses.

Well, maybe he could resolve them one way or the other. It was time — a vagueness of gray light had begun to stain the window. That was all he needed. If enough still remained of the tracks.

Moving in total silence, Sully lifted his blankets off and swung his sock feet to the floor. Fully dressed except for his boots, he felt for them by his bunk and pulled them on. His mackinaw and hat and a couple of wool scarves were ready to hand; he donned them, picked up his rifle, and slipped noiselessly as a cat across the bunkroom to the door. Opening and shutting it without arousing anyone would be the ticklish part. The latch creaked softly as he lifted it; he eased the door open just a foot. A soft gust of cold swept the room as he slid outside and swiftly closed the door.

So far, so good. Sully scanned the ground as he hurried to the stable, noting that the tracks trampled out a few hours before were still plain. But they'd blown over to shallow depressions and were filling fast; the wind was picking up. No time to lose. Glancing toward Mrs. Ekstrom's house, he saw a light in the window. She too had been roused by the excitement when Cyrus's body was discovered; she knew that Bowie Candler was missing. Sully wasn't sure what-all had developed between Bowie and her, but he guessed it ran deep enough that she too would be getting little sleep this night.

Entering the stable, Sully located and lighted the bull's-eye lantern. By its sickly light he quickly saddled and bridled his favorite horse, a sturdy short-coupled pinto. In a few minutes he was on the open flats north of headquarters, riding briskly. The snow hadn't deepened enough during the night hours to seriously impede him, but here on the flats wind and snow had conspired to all but erase the horse tracks. Two horsemen had ridden this way; one had returned. Sully was soon convinced that Brady had lied about following Candler's tracks a short distance. The tracks of both horses continued far onto the flats. Brady hadn't followed Bowie this far in the storm unless he was right with him, Sully knew.

Though still held to guesswork, he was beginning to fear the worst.

In places the tracks had drifted completely over. Time and again Sully was forced to go slowly, keeping on a straight line and hoping; each time he did, his calculations were rewarded. Here and there, where a bank or swale had broken the drive of wind and snow, tracks still showed faintly. Before long he was climbing an old trail into a belt of pines which had sheltered the light prints so well that sign of two horses, one following the other, told a plain story. *Only one rider had returned.*

More and more Sully felt chilled by the implications: Bowie didn't know the landscape well enough to cut string-straight for this ridge trail in a storm. But Brady did. Brady had been in control; he'd deliberately herded Bowie in this direction.

The light was steadily growing, the storm still holding low. As he advanced into the timber and it closed behind him, Sully hipped around in his saddle without drawing rein. Scanning his backtrail was an instinctive precaution; he didn't expect to see anything.

His heart gave a sickening jolt. A rider was following him. Scarcely more than a faint shadow on the murky scape, he was holding a good distance. But unmistakably he was on Sully's trail.

Brady hadn't been sleeping either, Sully guessed bleakly. Had he kept a watch from the house on the chance that somebody would try to pick up the fading trail that would prove him a liar? No matter. He saw me ride out, Sully thought with conviction, and he knew why.

Deep in the trees now, Sully pulled up behind some clustering pines and dragged his Springfield from the saddle boot. All he need do was sit his horse offside the trail and wait. Snow flurried down through the branches in wicked gusts; he had the bone-deep feeling that this slow building storm would be smashing down with blizzard force before very long.

He heard the rider coming up through the trees; then he swung abruptly into view. Sully lifted his rifle and crossed the rider's chest with his sights. "You — stop there!"

Even as he spoke, he saw with surprise that this wasn't Brady. It was Sofie Ekstrom, firmly astride a man's saddle with her skirt bunched tight around her legs against the cold. She looked lost inside a bulky mackinaw; tendrils of her hair blew free of the scarf knotted over it.

"Mr. Calder? You do not shoot, please."

Sully clucked his tongue in disgust and rode down to her, reining up by her stirrup to stirrup. "God almighty, Miz Ekstrom, what you think you're about?"

"The same you are, I think." She blinked against the snow gusts; her face was pink with cold. "I watch from my window when you ride out. You do not believe Mr. Brady Trapp, eh?"

"Miz Ekstrom, you better turn that nag around and get back fast as you can. This weather'll be turning a sight worse directly."

"*Ja.* Maybe I know winters better than you, eh? That's why I come after you. If Mr. Candler's somewhere hurt, he will need good care. I have brought some stuff will help. Did you think of this?"

"We don't know anything for sure yet," Sully snapped. "I can't have you dragging along and time's growing short. Don't argue with me."

"I do not argue." Her tone was quiet, her jaw stubborn; worry overlay her face like an angry shadow. "I am going with you. Do not waste time, go on now. I follow you."

Swearing softly, Sully gigged his horse onward, through the last trees and onto a steep ridgeside where black bulges of rock thrust up through patchy veins of snow. He could only hope to God that Brady had taken Bowie this way and that the trail would end soon. For on this high open slope, the wind had swept every vestige of their tracks clean away.

Bowie dragged his eyes open. He couldn't see much of anything and he felt nothing at all. He moved a hand; it felt like a chunk of ice. So did his whole arm as he raised it and brought the hand to his face. Like ice touching ice. Jesus! He lifted his head and forced his arms and legs to move; he sat up. Shattering pain in his head. The whole right side of his face was numb where it had rested on the snow. He gazed stupidly at the bloody claws of his hands. Then he began to remember.

He climbed to his feet; snow sifted from his clothing. He took a tottering step and nearly fell. Stood dizzy and swaying, trying to collect his senses. Feeling started to flood back to most of his battered body. A multitude of bruises quivered to life; agony tore midway at his legs. Clothes ripped all to hell, pants and underwear shredded to bloodied tatters at the knees. Bowie batted clumsily at the numb side of his face, feeling a thrust of panic now as he realized that he could hardly feel his hands or feet. He braced his trembling legs and forced himself to take one slow step, then another, setting his teeth. He could walk; could he move his fingers? He forced them to curl against his palms. He could hardly tell that he had toes, but they wiggled. Nothing was broken, nothing frozen.

He strode up and down stamping his feet, beating his arms against his sides. Gathered up a handful of snow and rubbed it vigorously over his face; it helped clear his head. Burning sensation prickled sharply into ears and toes. Bowie felt a mighty surge of relief. Touch of frostbite, nothing worse. His palms and knees had been savaged raw in his descent of the rugged gorge flank, but the stabbing pain was actually welcome. His head seemed to balloon with a crushing pulse of pain, but running a hand over it, he found only a swollen knot behind his ear. The skin hadn't even been broken.

He halted by the crumpled body of the buckskin. The sloping wall and thin cushion of snow that had saved Bowie's life hadn't benefited the horse. He'd plunged down in a straight battering fall that was unbroken till he'd hit the flint-edged fragments of fallaway rock that littered the gorge floor. Bowie crouched down, brushed away some mounding snow, and laid a hand on the still warm flank. Neck broken. Spine probably severed clean and instantly. One break for you, old Shitkicker. You were a good one. Bowie's eyes stung; he felt a rise of seething rage.

God damn Brady Trapp. God damn his meeching dirty soul to hell.

Had to see to getting out of this place. He hadn't a notion of how long he'd been unconscious, but it was still dark. The weather hadn't appreciably worsened in the interval; he was pretty well sheltered from the wind here. But the storm could pick up fiercely any time, the relatively light cold plunging much lower. He'd be all right while he kept moving about, but the main thing was to find a way out of here.

Bowie scanned the walls of the gorge up and down, squinting against the darkness and eddying flakes. Both the flanking slants were so steep that he doubted he could climb either side. No rugged projections that he could make out, only rounded nubs of rock that his raw palms would be unable to grip.

Maybe he could follow the gorge to its end. Or at least to an easier point of ascent. He tramped about a hundred yards northward till he came to a dead end: the gorge boxed off in a sheer wall.

Retracing his steps down canyon, he found that the cleft narrowed steadily. Finally the walls pinched down to a crack he couldn't wedge his body through.

Jesus God. He was in a goddam trap.

A first real fear began to nettle Bowie's guts. No way out except up one treacherous wall or the other. And he was like to break his neck trying. What were the chances of someone being suspicious enough of Brady's explanations to backtrack him? Sully might do so, good chance that he would, but suppose the goddam tracks were covered up by morning? No — no odds in just waiting. Particularly when Brady himself might return by daylight to make sure of him.

Soon as there was light enough, he'd make the try. He whiled away the time tramping up and down, studying the walls. He could barely make out the rimrock, but he reckoned it to be some sixty feet above his head. He sized up a spot where he might be able to climb part way with the aid of a rope, at the same time taking note of a sizable bulge about halfway up. It just might block his further ascent, but he couldn't locate a likelier place to make the climb. Bowie got the lariat from his saddle and worked the cold-stiff coils in his hands as he walked, gritting his teeth against the agony of his palms.

The rimrock grew sharper against a slowly graying sky. Long minutes more passed before enough light reached into the gorge to pick out the separate heels of projecting rock. Bowie's rope was thirty feet long; he couldn't snag anything higher than halfway up. After considerable study, he settled on a fairly rough-edged spur just above the bulge. Be a tight cast even if his rope could reach it.

After a half-dozen throws, he looped his noose over the spur. Gathering the shreds of his will, he gripped the rope tight in both raw hands and swung his full weight on it. The effort was excruciating, but the noose was securely fixed; the spur itself held firm.

Agonizingly, slowly, he began going hand over hand up the precarious slant, using his feet all he could to take some of the savage pressure off his hands. Pebbly fragments rattled away from under his rasping boots. Sweat crawled down his forehead and half blinded him. Holding on briefly one-handed, Bowie brushed it away with his sleeve. Climbed on. He felt a sharpening alarm when pain began to subside because his hands were going numb. Worms of blood crawled warmly down his wrists, slicking his tortured grips on the jerking line. He could feel the creeping weakness in his fingers.

A little farther — just a little. Then he could rest a minute.

Several feet below the obstructing bulge was a rugged knob broad enough to offer footholds. At last, unable to see for the reddening haze on his vision, Bowie halted and groped with his feet. Felt the knob solidly beneath them. Cautiously relaxed his straining holds as he let the projection take his full weight. It held. Rubbery and trembling in every muscle, he leaned hard against the wall, supporting himself with a light grip on the rope.

Almost halfway. But Jesus. Did he have enough left to pull himself to the spur where his noose was anchored? If he did, how would he get the leverage to cast it over a higher projection — if he could locate one? Bowie settled his chin wearily on his chest. Nothing to do but rest a while, and then try calling on a reserve of strength he wasn't sure he possessed. His teeth began to chatter as the chill of immobility ate into his flesh.

Something off key touched his dulled nerve ends. Sounds that weren't a part of the gaunt dawn or the whispering snow.

At first he thought he'd imagined them. Shook his head to clear it and listened. Faint voices carrying on the low wind — one a woman's. At least two people. Bowie called, "Here," his voice a husky croak.

A moment later they edged into view on the rim above. For a moment he couldn't quite believe it, yet who else might he have expected? Nobody, of course. Nobody but Sully and Sofie.

"How you doing, paleface?" Sully called.

"I could use another rope if you got one."

"That's what we got. One."

Sully pulled back from sight. Reappeared with his coiled catch rope. Dropping its noose end over the rim, he paid out line till it dangled a couple feet above Bowie's head. "That's all she'll run," Sully said. "Wait a minute." He stretched out on his belly and extended his arm downward, gripping the rope end. The noose brushed Bowie's shoulder. Slowly and awkwardly, hardly able to work his finger, he crudely tied it to his own rope.

"You pull 'em both up and make a good hitch knot, we'll have more'n enough."

"You can hold on?" Sofie said anxiously.

Bowie hugged the cliff, his bloody palms flat against the icy rock. Now supporting his whole weight, the knob under his feet felt abruptly slick and precarious. "Sure. Haul away."

Sully swiftly drew both ropes up to the ledge, jerking Bowie's noose free of the spur. He tied the rope ends together with a series of hitches which he knotted in at several places. Again he dropped a noose to Bowie, this time with plenty of slack to spare. "Fasten that under your arms and hold on tight as you can. My horse'll pull you up."

The rest was comparatively easy. Sully hooked the rope over a rounded jog on the rimrock's lip, then backed his horse far enough onto the ledge trail to secure its end to the pommel. Mounting, he heeled the animal gently into motion. Bowie let his weight swing out, hanging briefly free over the long drop till he was dragged past the overhead bulge. From there on his body bumped gradually up the rough slant to the rim. Sofie was waiting, her strong hands reaching down to grasp his wrists. A moment later he was heaved up bodily onto the rim.

Utterly spent, Bowie stayed on his knees as Sofie lifted the rope off. His muscles felt like cold jelly. Sully came hurrying up. With the two of them supporting Bowie between them, they edged back single file along the narrow trail to safe ground.

CHAPTER FOURTEEN

Bowie should have shelter and warmth; he needed tending to. And the sooner he got them, the better. Brady was in control at Chainlink now, and the other nearest ranch outfit was miles away. That was how Sully summed it up. Best place to go, he said, was a line camp on Chainlink's high summer range north of here. It was deserted for the winter and it wasn't too far. But the storm was worsening as dawn advanced, so they'd best waste no time.

With Bowie on Sully's paint horse, Sully tramping ahead and Sofie bringing up the rear, they circled off the jag of ridges and swung north into a gentle rise of foothills. Sully led the paint, for it was all Bowie could do to hang on with his knees clamping the horse's barrel and his torn hands gripping the pommel. Sofie had ripped up some flannel rags to tie around his hands and Sully had pulled his own thick-fleeced gloves over them. They felt as if the nerves had been flayed bare; a fiery pulse quivered in every finger. Bowie knew if he relaxed his hold for a moment, he'd fall off.

The terrain had a feel of getting higher and more rugged. Despite the light of new day, the snow was blowing harder and thicker; you couldn't make out objects beyond a few yards away. Sully tramped steadily and surely against a wind that cut like blades off the heights. Most of Bowie's face was muffled in a scarf that Sully had provided; spikes of cold drove against every inch of his exposed skin. Cold seeped through his clothes and ate deeper into his already chilled flesh. His ears echoed with the wind's howl. His thoughts kept raveling away except for one: hang on and ride it out.

He didn't know how long the journey lasted. Minutes or an hour — maybe longer. He knew that Sully angled onto a high twisting trail; dark stands of pine marched by in the pelting whiteness. Here and there the trail would level out and then climb some more. Several times Bowie felt his hands slipping. Somehow dredged up the reserves of will to make his fingers tighten again. But he couldn't keep it up forever, before much longer he would weaken, he would fall. . . .

Suddenly the wind was cut off. He knew that first of all. Then Sully was saying words that jumbled senselessly in his ears. He raised his head blindly. A dimness of shed walls enclosed him; the paint horse had halted. Sully's hands tugged at him and Sofie was there too, helping ease him down to a stable floor. His legs gave way; they had to hold him upright, Sully saying: "Just a few yards, boy, you'll be all right, move your legs, that's it —"

Being able to move again, tramping upslope through deepening snow, wind fierce on his face, revived Bowie's sluggish senses. But he felt exhausted, bone tired, weary to the marrow. A long low building of peeled logs took form ahead and then they were in the lee of it, out of the wind, and Sully was unlatching a warped door, heaving his weight against it till the stiffened rawhide hinges bent and it scraped open. They pushed into a dark drafty room.

Bowie sagged gratefully onto a straw-tick bunk. Sofie found blankets and heaped them over him. Sully went back to tend the horses and fetch an armload of wood. He laid a fire in the field-stone fireplace and built it to a roaring blaze. It washed the time-darkened walls with a mellow glow and picked out the rough comforts of a puncheon table and benches, two bunks built into the cabin corners, and pantry shelves lined with crocks and utensils.

Sully made several more trips for wood till a sizable pile of oak lengths was stacked by the fireplace. Meantime Sofie rummaged among the shelves; she found a shallow pan and a coffeepot, filled both with snow, set the pan by the fire and hung the coffeepot on the fireplace lug. When the pan water had melted and warmed, she washed Bowie's lacerated hands and knees, treated them with bluestone and sweet oil she'd brought, and carefully tied them up with more rag bandages.

Sully dumped a final load of wood, unbuttoned his coat, and held his palms to the fire. "You thawed out yet, paleface?"

"Just about."

The fire's spreading warmth was nesting

nicely around Bowie's body. When the coffee was ready, he sat up in the bunk and cradled a steaming cup between his bandaged hands, sipping it slowly. They exchanged stories and offered each other speculations. Came to a few cautious conclusions, though some things still weren't clear.

"Up to you what you want to do now," Sully said. "You can cut across the peaks to K-town. That's if the storm lets up soon. Another day of it and the high passes'll be closed for the winter. But you been across that country and know the way. Barring a heavy snow, you can make it."

"But better he should go back and tell his story," Sofie objected. "Otherwise Brady Trapp gets away with all he did, eh?"

Sully filled a cup for himself. "Yes, ma'am, I reckon. Bowie's the only one who can tell the right of what happened. You and me, we can back up part of his story. We all go to Sheriff Beamis and tell him all, including how Brady stole his pa's cattle, I'd say we can stop Brady square in his tracks."

"Depends what sort of man the sheriff is," Bowie said.

"His own. I know him pretty well. He and Cyrus was life-long friends; Beamis knows what a cross-dog pup Brady is, too. You'll get more'n a fair hearing. Anyway you'll want to clear up it wasn't you stuck that pitchfork in Cyrus. Even allowing self-defense, it could mean a manslaughter charge."

Bowie nodded and yawned. He was snug as toast in a cocoon of blankets, but every ache and bruise twitched to his slightest movement. "Sounds all right," he said drowsily. "Should be fit enough to head for Saltville in a day or so. You two best get back to headquarters. But listen, you watch out for Brady. He'll guess what's up."

Sully flicked an unpleasant grin. "Let him guess. His tail's in a nice tight crack. Let him sweat it. He won't dare a damn thing. And I'll open his gizzard for him if he tries."

"Just be careful. You better tell Faye Nevers what's happened."

Sally scowled into his coffee cup. "I don't know as it's smart to tell Nevers anything."

"Why not?"

"Just a feeling. He's an off ox — you never know what's ticking in his head. Now Brady's in, he could just be out."

"What's bad about that? Puts him on our side."

"Might not be that simple. I suspicion Faye has got a stew of his own in the cooking. My sister told me that Faye and Miz Trapp have been carrying on a private thing for a good while now."

Bowie raised his brows. "She sure of that?"

"Tula don't miss much that goes on around the place. Yeah, she's sure."

"I think this is right," Sofie said quietly. "I have seen them together. It goes on a long time now. I do not think Mr. Trapp knew."

Sully laughed sardonically. "You can lay bottom dollar he didn't. Did he, ol' Faye would have got decked out for a shotgun funeral."

He inspected the pantry shelves and shook his head. "Coffee's about all that's laid in here saving some jerky strips that'll be tougher'n old whangs. I better fetch up some grub. You got everything else you need." As he spoke, Sully buttoned his coat and pulled on his gloves. "Listen to that wind. Tearing up a blue streak. We better get going, Miz Ekstrom, or we'll be riding out a real blizzard."

Sofie shook her head. "I stay here," she said firmly, her eyes on Bowie. "He needs looking after."

Sully smiled. "Well, maybe so. You suit yourself." He tramped to the door, saying over his shoulder, "Will be back shortly with that grub unless the weather turns a sight worse."

Faye Nevers had no concern about being seen as he crossed to the big haybarn. The snowy gusts had turned to a full-fledged blizzard that cut off visibility beyond a few yards. His mental map of the whole headquarters guided Nevers unerringly to the barn. His outstretched hand slapped against its wall now, and he felt along it to the small side door. Lifting the latch, he pushed inside and then jammed the door shut against the deafening howl of wind.

Blinking in the hay-musty dimness, he said, "Adah?"

A quick dark movement and she was in his arms, pressing close, her mouth hot and eager. Then she drew back, smiling ruefully. She was muffled in a black hooded traveling cloak; cold stung her face with fresh color. "Seems I've waited hours — not really, but it seemed so. Then the blizzard picked up and I was frightened — till just now. I don't believe I could find my way back to the house."

"Couldn't help being late." He took off the scarf that tied down his hat, then the hat itself, and batted both free of snow. "We had to move some weak stock back to shelter in the east draws before the big storm broke. It's a stemwinder, all right."

Adah pressed herself to him again, burying her face against his coat. Nevers moved his hands down the sleek curve of her back, but his thoughts were barely on the woman in his arms, a woman who ordinarily enflamed him with a look or touch.

Cyrus's death, though he'd been braced for it, had come as a stunning blow to Nevers. He felt nagging and angry doubts about how Cyrus had met his end; the flaws in Brady's telling had been only too apparent. Sully Calder must have thought so too, for he'd been gone this morning, evidently to strike out on his friend Candler's trail. All Nevers had done was dispatch a crewman to bear the news to Sheriff Beamis in

215

Saltville; what else could he do?

Actually he felt little interest in the *how* of Cyrus's death. All that really mattered was that he was gone. That Faye Nevers's whole future suddenly rested on a precarious footing. Whatever happened next might depend on a lot of things. But one thing was certain: nothing would be the same as it had been.

"I shouldn't be happy," came Adah's muffled murmur. "How can it be right at such a time? But I am happy! Now there's nothing to keep us apart. Nothing —"

"Sure." Stroking her back almost absently. "Sure . . ."

Adah tipped up her face, slipping back the hood. "And you're not a bit happy, are you? But I don't think it's Cyrus — what is it, Faye?"

He smiled crookedly. "Oh, just wondering if I'll have a job shortly. Any old thing to support a wife on."

She half smiled. "You've told me there's bad blood between Brady and you. But it's the same between Brady and almost anyone, isn't it? He'll still need a foreman, and he's not likely to find a better."

"You don't know Brady." Nevers glumly shut his jaws. He eased himself into a pile of crackling hay and pulled her down beside him. "The final word'll come from Cyrus's will. I'd give a pretty penny to know what it is."

She gave him a surprised look. "Why, I can tell you that."

216

In his tormented last days, Adah said, Cyrus had been moved to share some of his thoughts with her. He'd wrestled long and hard with this particular dilemma, but once made, his decision had been firm. No matter what else they might be, Brady and Joe-Bob were his sons. His will as it was already filed would stand: full control of Chainlink would go to Brady. Cyrus's one hope had been that Brady's impulsive vigor would refocus and steady under the pressure of responsibility. If that hope didn't materialize, the fate of Chainlink was of no consequence; he'd built up this place for his sons and their sons to come. Brady would see after Joe-Bob; Cyrus had no concern on that score. As for Adah, she would be handsomely provided for, well enough to permit her to return to Denver and make a comfortable life, which was all that she really cared about.

"It's what I *did* want, Faye," she murmured. "All I want now is to be with you — wherever or however it pleases you."

Nevers had listened to her recital with mounting impatience. "That's fine, honey. But answer me something if you can. Didn't he have a word for me in all this?"

Adah showed an uncertain little smile. "Well — the will does advise Brady to retain you as foreman."

He stared into her face. "*Advises* — that's all?"

"Cyrus said that he didn't want to leave any hard and fast restrictions on Brady's behavior. He'll have to make all his own decisions, wise or foolish. No other way to bring out whatever mettle he might have. And —" Adah paused, worrying her underlip between her teeth.

"All right, what?"

"He — Cyrus didn't trust you, Faye. He told me it was nothing personal. That he couldn't ask for a better foreman. But he was afraid of — well, the ambition he saw in you. Said he feared what might happen if you ever got the littlest toehold on Chainlink."

"He did, did he?"

"Oh, darling, I told him it was nonsense. But he only gave me that dreadfully sardonic look of his. It was useless to argue."

Nevers stared blindly at a wall.

So this was it. His reward. For years of ramrodding Chainlink better than any damn outfit in the territory was ramrodded. Cyrus had admitted that no small part of Chainlink's prosperity was owing to Faye Nevers. Not that he'd ever had illusions that Cyrus might think of him as a son, any crap of that sort. But he'd given the outfit the best years of his life and every drop of his loyalty.

And now. Jesus. A legacy of zero. With Brady in the saddle, it would come to that. The knowing congealed around his guts like ice.

"Faye," Adah whispered.

Nevers's eyes moved to her face. Saw a shadow in it edging on fear. He cleared his expression with a smile and a shrug. "Seems that's how it is then, honey. Let's forget about it. Like you say, we got each other. . . ."

Bowie slept for several hours. When he woke, it was plain that Sully wouldn't be returning to the line camp today. The blizzard was hammering at the house in full fury. The building trembled; the wind knifed between wall logs where the clay chinking had fallen out. Sofie plugged such gaps as she could locate with wads of cloth and paper, but the wind leaked through unseen cracks, making the place miserably drafty, wildly guttering the fire. She had to constantly replenish it to keep the room just above freezing.

Bowie broke a long silence. "Don't reckon you'll be welcome at Chainlink after this."

"No, I don't think so." She sat on the other bunk with her coat and a couple of blankets wrapped around her. "When you leave here, I go with you to Saltville. Later I send to Chainlink for my stuff, eh?"

"Sure. What then?"

"I must find work — work of some kind." Shadow and firelight played on Sofie's face; it looked indrawn and sad. "What kind of man is he, Brady Trapp? Did he kill his pa?"

"Maybe by accident. Like how he claimed I done it. No saying for sure what led up to it."

"Cyrus Trapp was very good to me. Why does a good man die like this?"

"Don't have to be a reason. No reason to much of anything else in life."

"Does it seem so?" She moved her head

slowly. "I can't believe that. I hope there is something."

"God, maybe?"

"For some people there is God, Bowie. For some there is very much God. . . ."

The hours passed. Bowie drifted in and out of sleep, running a slight fever. Gradually he became aware that the blizzard was bucking itself out, the wind no longer shrieking and yammering like dying horses. That it was growing dark outside, the room filling with deep shadow as the fire ebbed to cherry glimmers. And vaguely, that Sofie went out and came back many times with armloads of wood from the kindling pile under the eaves, clattering them on the floor by the hearth.

Bowie woke with a jerk. It was uncomfortably warm; sweat dewed his face and damped his whole body under the blankets. Sofie had stoked up the fire; the room was bright with steady firelight and heavily warm now that the drafts had died down. His confused, half-shuttered gaze found Sofie. She had thrown off her snow-caked coat; she sat on a bench peeling off her long black stockings, which had gotten wet in the wood-fetching. She worked her cotton drawers off from under the skirt and then, moving over to the hearth, hung the damp garments on the mantel to dry.

Stepping back, she gazed at the fire a moment. Then she bunched her skirt and camisole in one hand, holding them high as she slowly turned against the heat, warming her bare legs. After a moment, still turning, she went up on tiptoe, murmuring with pleasure. Beating firelight made a tawny shimmer on the smoothly beautiful legs, golden-fleshing her round and sturdy thighs, the flexing curves of her calves. Shadow undercupped her big breasts; it limned her young full body with an incredible witchery.

He tried to shut his eyes. Couldn't. Kept them clear open and watching till her gaze crossed his. She became motionless, looking at him; she let the skirts fall from her hand.

"Bowie — oh, Bowie." Whispering it.

He dimly felt that he should be surprised. He had never dared hope for anything like this. Not so that he'd consciously realized it. Yet he must have admitted something to a hidden half of himself. For now, as she came over and slipped into his arms, it seemed as easy and natural a thing as he'd known. . . .

CHAPTER FIFTEEN

Brady had Faye Nevers come to his father's office because this was where Cyrus and the foreman had often discussed matters of ranch routine. Arrogantly slacked in Cyrus's swivel chair, his crossed boots cocked on Cyrus's desk, Brady gave Nevers orders for the usual rounds of winter work: on riding line, on keeping the waterholes open, on feeding the bulls and weaker stock. Faye knew better than anyone exactly when and how all such work should be carried out; that fact was the source of the wicked pleasure Brady felt in seizing a position from which he could needle Faye with superfluous commands. Faye had made him sweat when the old man had set him under the foreman's thumb; now Faye would sweat. But as always, it was hard to be sure what Faye was thinking. He leaned his big-shouldered frame against the wall with arms crossed, listening, making no comment. Melting snow puddled around his boots.

"That's about it," Brady said, folding his hands behind his head. "Any questions?"

"Just one. I always figured the day you come in, I'd be out."

Brady chuckled. "We don't know who's in or out yet, now do we? Not till the old man's will is read — and the only copy we know of is filed with his attorney in Saltville. Safest thing for you to assume is that *I'll* get the whole outfit, lock, stock, and barrel. But hell, you know that."

"Not what I asked."

"I tell you, fella —" Brady leaned forward, thumping his boots to the floor. "You're likely to be guessing about it for a long spell to come."

Nevers's veiled stare narrowed slightly. He said nothing, just waited.

"Yessir," Brady said cheerfully, "if the old man's will don't get thrown into probate, I will be the big cheese around here damn shortly. Then I'll have you right by the balls, won't I, friend?"

"You waited for it long enough," Nevers observed dryly. "But what's it going to mean?"

"Why, just that I can keep you on as foreman if I want. Or fire you if it suits me. Any goddam time it suits me. Y'know, Faye? I can see where wondering on something like that could drive a fellow right up a tree."

A wicked glint of anger flicked out of Nevers's pale eyes. It made Brady sharply aware of what he didn't intend to forget: that Faye Nevers could be a dangerous man. "Don't crowd me too hard," Nevers said gently. "You'll find that has its limits."

Brady grinned lazily. "Why, hell, Faye, I got more sense'n to do that. But you gonna be walking soft from now on too. You sweated your ass too long and hard working up to what you got here at Chainlink to just turn on your heel and walk away from it all."

"That's right. Just don't make a mistake how much I'll take off you or any man."

"Sure." Brady smiled. "Don't worry."

Wordlessly Nevers clamped on his hat and went out. Brady rose and walked to the window, watching Faye head for the cookshack where the crew was at breakfast. The point was made, Brady thought, the knife slipped in with a deft twist: an unvarnished threat that without warning, at any time of his choosing, he could yank everything from under Faye. No need for a reminder, ever. From now on Nevers would live with that bitter knowledge; it would eat at his guts like corrosion. The thought filled Brady with a wicked pleasure. For the present he needed Faye; he had no illusions about stepping cold turkey into his father's boots. He had a lot to learn, all he'd neglected to absorb through a profligate youth. But all that was going to change. And the time would come.

If. One continuing worry nagged Brady as he gazed out at the snow-smoothed rollaway of the valley floor. Had Cyrus ever carried out his occasional threat to have a new will drawn up? Brady mused narrow-eyed on the ominous possibilities of such a development. Swore in a vicious undertone at his own lack of diplomacy in dealing with the old man those last weeks. But he felt a steely resolution too, which kind of surprised him. Seemed like the old man's death had freed him of an oppressive presence that had always cowed and weakened him.

That was done with, by God. He could do any damn thing he wanted now. Any damn thing necessary to cinch his control of Chainlink.

Beamis. The sheriff might be a problem. Yet what could he finally prove? Nothing. Candler's mouth was shut for good; only he and Joe-Bob knew the truth. Yesterday's blizzard had erased any last trace of sign left by his and Candler's horses. It would have buried the bodies of Candler and the buckskin under inches of snow, not to be discovered till spring and maybe not then. If the remains were ever found, it would be assumed that Candler had blundered over the rimrock in his flight.

Suspicions, sure. Be a barrelful of suspicions. But let anyone prove a goddam one of 'em.

Brady watched the crew ride out to their duties, then opened a drawer of his desk and took out a bottle and water glass. He filled the glass to the brim and drank off a third of it. Ahhh — good by God to be able to drink when and where he pleased in his own home. He toasted his new freedom with another deep swig.

"Excuse me —"

Brady lowered his glass and glowered at Adah standing in the open office doorway. She was pointedly eying the glass, disapproval cold in her voice and her composed face, which contrasted palely with the mourning black she wore.

A vicious irritation welled up in him. "Goddammit, can't you knock?"

"The door was open —"

"All right, all right! What the hell is it?"

"I want to discuss arrangements for the burial. You can spare a minute or two for that."

" 'Arrangements for the burial,' " he said in savage mimicry. "Nothing to it. Tell one of the boys to chop a hole in the ground and drop the old bastard in it. Or leave him in a barn till spring. He'll keep."

Adah's face had delicately colored; now all the color ran out of it. She moved her head slowly back and forth. "I — I can't believe that even you could be so, so utterly bestial, so callous —"

"Ah, Christ. Get out of here." He flung out his hand with the glass, sloshing liquor on his wrist. "G'wan," he roared, "get t'hell out!"

Adah wheeled and was gone. He heard her quick steps on the stairs. Muttering, he refilled the glass and drained it in a couple of swallows. Walking over to the window again, he stared out at the widow Ekstrom's cabin some hundred yards distant.

A new thought flicked at his hotly savage mood; more than whiskey began to stoke his innards. Abruptly he lifted his mackinaw off a wall peg, shrugged it on, and left by the outside door.

Tramping toward the cabin, he wasn't quite sure what approach he might take to back up the hot impulse boiling in him. Only that one way or another, he meant to have Sofie Ekstrom. Be diplomatic about it, sure, but make her understand who was running this outfit now. She'd either come to taw or get that nice round ass of hers booted off Chainlink.

Even before he reached the cabin, Brady's whiskey-fuddled mind cooled to attention on something that seemed damn funny. Not a trace of smoke coming from the chimney. The widow, usually an early riser, should have laid her breakfast fire a good hour ago, particularly on so cold a morning. No tracks showed outside the door; snow had drifted up against it.

Frowning, Brady rapped his knuckles on the door. No answer. He lifted the latch and stepped inside. The cabin was deserted. And cold. He went to the fireplace and touched the ashes. Dead for hours. But how long had she been gone? Before the blizzard had ended, that was sure. Bedclothes mussed, but everything else neat as a pin. Which indicated that she'd likely left at night and, for some reason, in haste. Also her disappearance could explain the horse that had been discovered missing after the storm.

But last night or the night before? Come to think of it, she hadn't been out and around all yesterday. Damn strange, that, unless she'd left Chainlink the same night that Cyrus had died — the night he had taken care of Candler. She and Candler'd been thick, all right. *Suppose she'd followed those tracks come morning?* Before the real blizzard had hit. Yeah . . .

Sudden fear made a phlegmy knot in Brady's throat. Might be a handy idea to ride up to the gorge where he'd left Candler and make sure. That was all he had to worry about. That

Candler might be alive. In the darkness and storm night before last, unable to see to the gorge bottom, he'd reckoned it a safe assumption that even if Candler had survived the plunge into the gorge or escaped being too busted up to move, there was no way he could climb out. He was sure to be froze to death by now.

Unless someone had helped him out. Christ!

Five minutes later Brady was throwing his saddle on his big grullo, having returned to the house just long enough to get his rifle. He rode north from headquarters, goaded by a feverish haste as he bucked the grullo savagely against a foot of drifted snow, breaking trail.

From a kitchen window of the big house, Sully and Tula watched Brady head northward. Turning her dark quick glance on her brother, Tula said, "He'll go to that gorge. What will he do when he doesn't find Candler in it?"

Sully smiled thinly. "Think on it a spell. Then figure what I did. Nearest shelter outside of headquarters 'ud be that old line camp. Get that grub together, sis. I got to hustle up there before Brady does."

"But he'll be ahead of you."

"Huh-uh. He'll go to the gorge first. There's a shorter way from here to the line camp. I'll lay up on the trail for him."

Concern shadowed her gaze. "Take care, Sully."

"Don't worry. Verily, sis, no Trapp is gonna

deadfall this Injun. Get the grub ready."

Sully, who had the winter wrangler's job of breaking in ranch horses, keeping them fed and gentled through the winter months, hadn't ridden out with the crew. As soon as they had gone, he'd slipped quietly up to the house and told Tula to pack some grub which he'd fetch to the line camp for Bowie and Miz Ekstrom. Seeing Brady head for the Ekstrom cabin, they hadn't been hard put to guess his intent, or the furious conclusions he'd have reached on finding Miz Ekstrom gone.

When Tula had loaded a flour sack with bacon, beans, cold biscuits, and coffee, Sully said a hasty good-by and hurried to the stable. After saddling his paint and tying the grubsack to his pommel, he checked the action of his Winchester. Smooth as baby skin. Brady's mood would be downright savage; even if a man got the drop on him, he might be inclined to push a showdown.

Standing in the stable doorway, Sully peered across the snow flats in the direction Brady had gone. He was still in sight, a diminishing dot on the plain's sweeping whiteness. Sully waited minutes longer for a roll of high ground to cut him off. Not until Brady had dropped out of sight did he start away from headquarters, cutting toward the northeast at an acute angle away from the trail Brady had broken. By the time each of them reached the timbered foothills, their trails would have diverged widely.

The sun poked out of the overcast now and then, sheeting the flats in glittering white that made Sully's eyes ache. He was glad to leave them for the first rise of scrub-timbered ridges. The route he'd chosen to the line camp was the quickest way he knew to get there; it was also the roughest. After passing the first mild ridges, he came to the base of a giant hogback that towered below the first peaks. It was treacherously steep; its long rugged flank extended several hundred yards from bottom to crest. Thrusts of broken shale studded its glaring mantle of snow. But it was the quickest way up, and the trail to the line camp followed its crest. Brady, when he came this way, would take the easy switchback trails leading up from the east.

Sully rested his horse a minute, then put the animal into a lunging ascent of the slope. Powder snow and loose stones flurried away from the paint's driving hooves. When he'd covered two-thirds of the distance, Sully dismounted and rested his animal again. Wiping sweat from his face with his sleeve, he peered up the final stretch of deep-tilted slope. He'd have to tackle it on foot. Leading the paint, he resumed his steady climb. Soon his leg muscles ached and trembled with each slogging step. Sweat puddled his skin under his heavy clothes; a raw band of pain grew around his rib cage. His face felt brittle with cold as sporadic gusts of high wind raked the open slope.

At last, his heart pounding, Sully achieved the

stand of lodgepole pine that marked a rounding off to the ridge's flat crown. A few more yards and he would hit the line camp trail. In saddle again, he pushed swiftly through the timber. It was easy going here, the snow only inches deep, the bulk of it caked thickly atop the interlacing pine branches overhead, shrouding the forest aisle in a pale gloom.

Sully pulled up suddenly. A prickling feel of something not quite right rippled up gooseflesh on his back. What the hell was it? Something his senses couldn't quite catalogue. Listening, he heard only a low moan of wind. Scanning the trees and the snow barred by their pale blue shadows, he couldn't detect anything.

Nothing — of course. Hell, how could Brady get ahead of him?

Yet he eased his Winchester from its boot before he nudged the horse cautiously forward. Ahead now, he saw the half-drifted trail between the tree boles.

The only other thing he saw, and the last thing of all, was a flicker of dark movement among the pines just off the trail. He didn't even have time to draw rein before something slammed him in the chest with piledriver force. The first thunder of the shot touched his senses, but that single edge of awareness was already dimming as he fell.

Then there was darkness. And there was nothing.

CHAPTER SIXTEEN

Bowie paced the cabin floor in a slow circle, gingerly working his muscles while he chewed an extremely tough piece of jerked deermeat to bits of fibrous pulp that would slide down his throat. His hands and knees still hurt like hell; some of the worst bruises on his carcass would be a long time fading. Yet he figured he was in shape to hold a saddle. Anyway he was impatient to get to Saltville and have his powwow with the sheriff. If he had to eke out a couple more days on flinty jerky and weak coffee, he thought dourly, his belly would be playing tag wrassle with his backbone.

He walked to the bunk where Sofie was still sleeping, curled on her side. One deep hip mounded the covers; her pale hair fanned out on the rough tick. He slapped her hip gently. "Wake up. Daylight on the mountain."

Stirring, she twisted onto her back like a big lazy cat, stretching her bare arms. "Come here," she murmured. "Come down here. *Ja ar kall.*"

"Better get up if you're cold. It's halfway to noon. Got to be getting a move on if we're going to raise Saltville before dark."

She lifted on her elbows, her eyes sultry. "So late? It cannot be. I am yet so sleepy. . . ."

He grinned. "Well, you didn't get a lot of sleep. Come on, up. I'll get the horses ready, you put the fire out, all right?"

"Mmm. *Tack sa mycket.*" She stretched again, yawning. "But are you fit to ride?" Then laughed at her own question. "*Ja,* I think so. But we should wait for Sully, eh? Today he should come."

"No point waiting. We'll leave him a note."

She tossed the covers aside and rose. Began unself-consciously to dress, so that he delayed putting on his coat for the pure pleasure of watching her. Her long hair, a shining shawl on which firelight twinkled, covered her almost demurely to the waist. It swung to her slightest movement, showing flashes of pearly flesh, the firm rises of half-melon breasts, the pale pink of softened nipples that hours ago had flowered to fierce firepoints in the surging, timeless clasp of passion. It was still hard to believe. All of it was. *I never knew any man but Jan before,* she had told him, and he knew it was true and did not know how he knew. Nor why the wonder of it would stay with him always, for he knew that too. There might yet be a lifetime of times, but this shining first would isolate itself in some corner of memory that kept inviolate, strangely young.

She gave a peal of laughter. "Is that how you get the horses ready, you *dumskalle!*"

Grinning, he shrugged on his mackinaw and tramped outside, closing the door behind him. For a moment he stood gazing across the broad fallaway of land on all sides. Damn strange place for a line camp, perched on a high bulge of ridge off from much of anything, including good graze or water. Still, it commanded a hell of a view. Northward, great peaks grew into the low-banked clouds like squat wedges; their snow-veined heights greened with timber along the lower slopes, shading to dull buff and slaty grays above. To the south lay pine ridges and snow flats across which Bowie could see for miles, making out trickles of smoke from the house and cookshack at Chainlink headquarters. The sky was rapidly clearing; belts of sunlight raced below the wind-chased clouds.

Cold nipped at his ears as he trudged down the slope toward the horse shed with the little corral strung out behind it. Then he came to a dead stop. A man's booted tracks were freshly trampled in the snow fronting the shed. But he saw them too late.

The unlatched shed door creaked as a hand nudged it open.

Brady Trapp stood just inside the doorway, a Remington-Keene rifle nested in the crook of his arm. Gripping both hands around the weapon now, he stepped out of the shed and began tramping upslope to where Bowie stood. Dull light raced along the tipped-up gunbarrel, which never wavered off Bowie's belly.

And Brady never stopped grinning.

He halted square in front of Bowie. "Hell, pilgrim. You didn't need to come down here. I was coming to you —"

The rifle swept up in one streaking vicious motion. Its barrel crashed against Bowie's neck.

Dark lights shattered in his eyes. Then he fell on his hands and knees, retching. And his head rocked and pounded to the endless roar of Brady's laughter.

Trying to feign being hurt worse than he was, Bowie sat hunched on the end of a bunk, elbows on his knees, gently rubbing the swollen side of his neck. He was sideways to Brady, but could see his reflection in the cracked bowl of a hurricane lamp. Brady's image swam grotesquely in and out of it as he stalked up and down the room, restlessly bouncing his rifle in the circle of his fist. He kept talking a blue streak, punctuated with bursts of savage laughter.

Now he was telling them how he'd concealed his horse back in the timber before stealing up to the line camp. Not seeing tracks outside the cabin, he'd looked in the horse shed to be sure. They'd have horses. And the horses were there; but just then the cabin door had opened as Bowie started coming out. Brady had swiftly pulled the shed door shut after him and then simply waited. Seemed he wanted to brag on and on. That was all right; it would hold off whatever he had planned for them. Which didn't take much figuring.

They had already absorbed the ugly shock of Brady's first brutal revelation: he had killed Sully. He'd also filled in the picture of how Cyrus had died.

Swallowing against sickness, Bowie watched

the warped leer of Brady's reflection, thinking with a kind of vague wonderment that he'd never seen this sullen man so feverishly jubilant. Not even at those times when he was riding a tight gamble in a poker game: the only thing that Bowie had seen lift his surly spirits to a similar boisterousness. And Bowie wondered: was this the same with him somehow?

Moving his head now, Bowie let the edge of his gaze touch Sofie's. She was seated on the bench by the table where Brady had ordered her to sit; her eyes followed him up and down the room. Scared, but not showing it much. The cold timbers creaked to Brady's heavy tramp; his glance flicked against their faces whenever he swung past one of them. He was enjoying hell out of this.

". . . sonofabitching breed wasn't as smart as he figured." Watching quick-eyed for their reactions as he talked. "Hell, it come to me halfway to that gorge where you'd be unless the widow got you out of it. Say she had —" Wheeling to a halt by the bunk, he gave Bowie a wicked prod with the rifle. "Only goddam place up here you was likely to go is here, right?"

"I never knew about this place," Bowie said in a dull voice. "Sully brought us here."

"I bet he did. Shit. I figured that out myself, after." Brady chuckled, resuming his clumping stride. "After I got the son of a bitch, that is. I never went to the gorge, switched northeast and cut straightway up here. Had got on the trail yonder along the hogsback when I hear this noise like someone's scrambling along up the side of it. Left my horse and got by the edge of timber, and yessir, it was old Sully, climbing up pert as you please. So I faded back a ways in the trees and laid myself up. When the bastard come in sight, I busted him clean."

The savage callousness touched a cold nerve of fury in Bowie. He forgot his injured pose. Raised his head and stared straight at Brady with a chill, voiceless hatred.

"He'd a done the same for me," Brady went on cheerily. "That's why he short-cut across country to get up here ahead of me. He'd a made it, too, if I hadn't thought me to cut straightway over to this old camp. Put me up here just a hair ahead of him. . . ."

He was like a gramophone that refused to run down. Rambling on about plans he had, dwelling on each detail. He didn't figure that getting rid of them with nobody the wiser would pose too much of a problem. All he had to do was dump their bodies into a convenient ravine, along with the breed. The three of 'em would keep well enough till spring, when he'd return and cover them more permanently. This first snow would melt down quickly in a day or two of sun; that would take care of tracks. Of course a lot of questions would be asked, but he'd have his trail covered all right; take more than three people dropping out of sight to get anything pinned on him.

Bowie was hardly listening. His head was pretty clear by now; keeping it lowered while he slowly massaged his neck, he focused everything on trying to think of a way out. He could make a dive for Brady any time Brady's pivoting stride carried him close, but there seemed little chance of completing it. Brady never swung closer to him than six or seven feet. Moreover, Brady was faster than his stocky-bull build might suggest, Bowie knew; he was in top condition and Bowie was still feeling the heavy punishment of two nights before. Also Brady had the rifle.

I need an edge, ran Bowie's tight thinking, any sort of edge. Whenever Brady's glance swiveled off from him, Bowie let his eyes move quickly over the room. Trying to discover anything that might help tip the balance. A hand ax which Sofie had used to split some of the larger chunks of firewood she'd carried in was sunk in a sizable piece she'd used for a chopping block. But the hatchet was a good fifteen feet away. Brady would easily cut him down before he reached it.

"How can you do so?" Sofie's voice cut passionately across Brady's ramblings. "Your pa first! Sully Calder then. Us now. You cannot just go on killing. What kind of poison is in you to think so?"

Brady looked surprised. He came to a halt and stared at her. "For a bitch who's been living on Trapp bounty all these weeks, you take on a Christawful lot of airs. What you got to be so goddam sniffy about anyway? Cozying your ass up here with this pilgrim —" A red smoldering flicked his gaze. "Maybe we should see what you got that's so great. Take it off."

"What?"

"Take your clothes off. Right now. Every goddam stitch!" Brady's voice was climbing; he leaned forward hard and then settled back on his heels. "Every stitch," he said gently.

Sofie shot a glance at Bowie. Then moistened her lips, gripping the edge of the bench with both white-knuckled hands. "I will not. You go ahead, you shoot. You cannot make me do this."

"Sure, I shoot," Brady said softly. He moved the rifle in a semi-arc till it covered Bowie. "I shoot that son of a bitch sitting over there first of all. Then I'll take your goddam clothes off myself. You like that idea better, just say so."

"No, no —" Her unbraided hair stirred to her quick shake of head. "I do what you want. Please —"

"That's better. I like you better scared." He motioned sharply with the rifle. "Get to it."

Sofie rose slowly to her feet. Her chin was up, her face white. She unbuttoned her coat and slipped it off, dropping it to the bench.

"Take your time." Brady's beard cracked in a goatish grin. "Just see you don't miss nothing."

She dropped to one knee to unfasten a shoe, her hair falling over to curtain her bent face. Brady watched avidly, his jaw hanging a little. Bowie felt the thinnest lift of hope now. Let Brady be distracted just enough. . . . But he was standing side-on to the bunk and could easily detect and stop any move Bowie made.

So he didn't go for the hatchet. Taking a long chance, he climbed shakily to his feet. Stumbled slowly toward Brady, saying hoarsely, "You bastard. Stinking bastard —"

Brady swung the rifle to cover him. "Now that's being purely stupid, pilgrim. I can drop you straightway any time it suits. Might's well relax and get your enjoyments out o' this. Gonna be your last."

Bowie lurched sideways in a loose stagger as if he'd gone off balance; it brought him close to one end of the fireplace. Grabbing at the mantel for support, he sagged there, watching Brady balefully.

Sofie straightened up, shaking back the white-flame veil of her hair. Slowly she flexed one leg, reaching down to one loosened shoe; it thudded on the floor. The other shoe followed. Her stockinged feet whispered on the rough boards. Then she reached for the neck of the rough hickory shirt she wore. Doing it all deliberately and without haste, never taking her eyes off Brady.

Bowie understood. Sofie was striving to give an extra edge to his chances. As he'd intended, his move to the fireplace had brought him inside four feet of the hatchet.

One quick reach, a twist to free the blade, a hard fast throw. Hell, he'd played throw-the-ax many times as a kid. Only throwing at a target painted on a broad stump. If you'd missed, the only forfeit had been a hooting by your opponent.

Be a sight steeper penalty here.

Sofie's fingers moved slowly down her shirt front, unbuttoning it to the waistband of her skirt. She pulled out the shirttail, unfastened two more buttons, slid out of the shirt, and let it fall from her hands. Lampglow washing through the gloomy room turned the creamy flesh of her shoulders and arms softly golden. The lace-edged camisole partly showed the pale mounds of her large firm breasts; lamplight filled the deep cleft between them with satiny shadow. Brady was leaning forward in his intensity, his underjaw slack; sweat sheened his cheekbones. The corners of Sofie's lips tilted softly upward as she watched him. Now she raised both hands to her shoulders and slipped the straps of her camisole downward. . . .

Bowie took just two swift steps sideways; his outwhipping hand closed on the ax and wrenched it from the block. Brady snapped partly around just as he swung the hatchet back and overhanded it in one savage motion.

Too low. The thought flashed across Bowie's mind even as the ax left his hand. Aimed at Brady's head, turning over once in flight, it was coming in shoulder level. And Brady desperately twisted his body at the last moment. The arcing blade sheared through his coat and shirt and then, deflected at an angle, glanced away and clattered to the floor.

As Brady still hung off balance, rifle pointed down, Bowie was already diving at him. Brady had just caught his balance and was turning on his heel, bringing his rifle up and around, when Bowie's head and shoulder slammed into his ribs under his right arm. Brady gave an explosive grunt, and then Bowie's impetus carried both men against the wall with an impact that shook the cabin.

Bowie clinched, trying to pin Brady to the wall while he grappled him for the rifle. But Brady held the weapon high, shifting his hold on it, then hammered the barrel down on Bowie's hunched back. Bowie's body arched in a spasm of pain; he let go and staggered backward. Brady pushed away from the wall, swinging the rifle up for a full-arm blow at Bowie's head. Beyond the red haze of his vision, Bowie saw Brady's crazed swollen face.

And in that instant, with Brady wide open, legs braced apart, Bowie put all his remaining strength into a quick, savage kick. Its power rippled out of the big muscles of his thigh and spurted the length of his leg into his straightened foot.

The toe of his boot drove square into Brady's crotch.

"Aaahh —"

A wounded roar burst from Brady's throat; his fingers splayed open in a reflex of pure agony. The rifle fell to the floor. Bowie took a stumbling step and then bent to snatch it up. But even half paralyzed with pain, Brady wasn't out of it. Before Bowie's hand could close on the rifle, Brady's heavy palm clapped against his neck, swung him in a powerful sideways heave, and flung him away. Bowie kited into a bench and overturned it, then tripped and fell across it. His ears ringing, he scrambled up on his knees and stayed that way a moment, gathering his strength.

Brady was half bent over, holding his groin, face twisted and bloodless. His whole right sleeve was wet red from the deep cut that the ax had opened in his shoulder. But even wounded, his eyes glazed with sick pain, he was still a formidable bull of a man: ape-squat and brutishly muscled, his body packed with the power of coiled spring-steel. To close with him again could be suicidal, a realization that cleared Bowie's head completely.

For this moment all that Brady could manage was to bend over, wheezing and holding himself. But in another moment he'd be able to pick up the rifle at his feet. Sofie stood by the bench as if gripped in a trance. Bowie's glance found the hatchet, which had skittered almost against her skirt hem. But there was no time to go after it, for abruptly Brady was bending deeper, reaching down for the rifle.

Bowie yelled *"Sofie — the ax!"* as he lunged at Brady again.

Already Brady was coming up with the

Remington-Keene, snapping its finger lever down. In the last straining instant Bowie batted wildly at the barrel, cuffing it aside as Brady pulled the trigger. The shot was thunderous in the room; crockery crashed and tinkled as the bullet whanged into the pantry shelves.

The two men struggled for the rifle, Brady still half hunched with pain. Bowie surged his weight backward, trying to wrest the weapon away. The effort yanked Brady forward off balance, but he kept his hold. Then Brady's plunging weight caused them to fall together, Bowie on the bottom. As his back hit the splintery floor, he tried to bring his knee up into Trapp's injured groin. But it only caught his hard-muscled thigh, and then Brady's bulk crushed him flat.

Bowie heaved upward, but Brady had him solidly pinned, and now Brady's hands were forcing the rifle down on his throat. Bowie put his last strength into holding it back, but the rifle began pressing into his throat with a crushing power. He felt his hold slipping.

A hard *tunk* like a mallet hitting a melon: Brady's snarling face went blank and he slumped across Bowie. Sofie stood over them, the hatchet poised in her fist. She'd brought the blunt heel of it down on Brady's head.

Bowie rolled Brady aside and then, with Sofie's help, climbed shakily to his feet.

"I could not kill him," she said simply.

He wanted to smile at that, but only managed to bare his teeth in a painful grimace. The short brutal encounter had wakened every bruise on his body to pulsing life. But he couldn't rest now. Not with the end of this in sight.

"We'll take him down to Saltville," he told Sofie. "We'll tell the sheriff all that's happened."

"I hope he will believe us. He must."

"Well" — Bowie did smile then — "when Brady got running off like molasses in July, he told quite a lot. Put it all together, I think we got a story the law will listen to."

CHAPTER SEVENTEEN

The sun was lifting fiercely past noon, making an eye-stabbing glare on the rapidly melting snow. It lay warm against Faye Nevers's right side and back as he swung the ax in hard measured strokes. He'd peeled off his mackinaw some time ago, but still his flannel shirt clung sweatily to his broad back.

Nevers liked the solid rhythm of this work, into which a man could throw his full muscle. Pausing, he wiped sweat from his forehead and glanced around the oak clearing to which he'd brought four of the crew on a wood-cutting detail. Barney too was swinging an ax, felling the scrub oaks and limbing them off; Hilo and Sam were bucking the logs into ten-foot lengths with a cross-cut saw; Trinidad was loading them onto the bed of a post wagon. The ring of axes and rasp of saw and clean resinous smell of fresh-cut wood all seemed to blend into one.

Trinidad topped the loaded wagon with an oak length, jammed it tightly into place, and glanced at Nevers. "She's pret' big load, Faye. You want me to drive her to headquarters now?"

"Yeah. Sully's there; tell him to help you unload. Then get back here double time. I want to get in three-four more loads today."

Trinidad was about to swing up the wagon seat. He paused and tipped his hat down, shading his eyes as he peered past the trees. "Someone comes. Looks like the kid. Joe-Bob."

It was. He came into the clearing on a lathered, hard-driven mount and dropped to the ground. Half stumbling, he went to Trinidad and grabbed him by the arm. "Trin, you gotta come with me!"

Trinidad stared at him and said: "What's 'at?" Then gave Nevers an uncertain grin.

Nevers set his ax down and tramped over to them. "I boss these men, kid, remember? You want Trinidad. What for?"

Joe-Bob swallowed, his eyes furtive and miserable. "I can't tell you nothing 'bout that, Faye."

"Sounds like something Brady don't want talked about. Is that right?"

Joe-Bob stubbornly shook his head. "I want Trinidad to come with me. You don't need to know any more."

Nevers glanced at Trinidad, who stood by hipshot, arms folded. "You know what he's talking about?"

The rawboned Mexican shrugged, his dark eyes veiled and amused. *"Quien sabe?"*

"Sorry, kid. I need him here."

Joe-Bob's milky eyes flared slightly. "Listen, Chainlink ranch will be part mine, Faye. You better not forget that."

"Let's wait till the will is read." Nevers smiled. He seated himself on a stump and cuffed back his hat. "Seeing you're the big augur here, they ought to listen to you. How about you, Trinidad? You listening?"

"Shee-yit, Faye." Trinidad showed a small cautious grin. "It's you gives the orders, ain' it? I ain' been told otherwise." He laid a hand on Joe-Bob's shoulder and said apologetically, "That's how she is, old *amigo*. Maybe you tell Faye what she is that is itching you, he leave me go with you, hah?"

"It ain't none of his mix, Trin!" Joe-Bob looked on the edge of tears. "I thought you was my friend."

"Why, shee-yit, boy, I ain' nothing else. But Faye here's my boss, tha's different. Anyway he only want to help you, ain' that right, Faye?"

Nevers half-lidded his eyes, nodding. "That's right, Joe-Bob. But I won't oblige a man who don't trust me."

"Brady don't like you," Joe-Bob said sulkily. "He don't like you any, Faye. He said so."

"Listen, Brady is wrong," Trinidad said sternly. "I am Brady's big *amigo*, but I say in this he is wrong. Faye Nevers done plenty for you Trapps, he helped make this Chainlink big and rich. Now you pa is gone, he is stick by you. And still Brady, he say he don' like Faye." The Mexican clucked his tongue sadly. "That is ver' bad way to pay a man who don' ask nothing but you be honest with him."

A kind of quizzical doubt crept into Joe-Bob's look. "I dunno," he muttered. "Might be all right. Brady didn't say about nothing like this — I gotta have some help."

248

"Look—" Nevers slid off the stump. "Nobody but the three of us needs to hear it. We can walk off a ways. How's that?"

"Yeah — I guess so."

Nevers waved the other men back to work. He led Joe-Bob and Trinidad deeper into the oak grove; they halted by a half-frozen creek. Joe-Bob's words spilled out almost frantically. From what Nevers could gather, Joe-Bob (not unusual for him) had overslept this morning and had gotten up to find Brady gone. He'd queried Adah, who'd told him that Brady had been acting peculiar; Brady had gone to Mrs. Ekstrom's cabin, afterward returning to the house to get his rifle, then hurriedly saddling a horse and riding off north. In a little while, what had seemed more peculiar, Sully Calder had left the house with what appeared to be a sack of food, had likewise gotten a horse and, after apparently waiting till Brady was out of sight, had ridden north too, but not the same way. Adah had seen it all from her upstairs window. Out of curiosity, then, she'd gone to the Ekstrom cabin and had been astonished to find Mrs. Ekstrom gone; she'd also questioned Tula, who wouldn't say a word. Adah had made no sense of it.

Neither did Nevers, but he was avidly alert now. "All right, kid," he said impatiently. "What's it all mean? Why'd you need Trinidad?"

"Brady could be in trouble, bad trouble. That breed is got it in for him, but Jeez, I'm no shakes with a gun. I can't do nothing. That's why Trin's

249

gotta help, but we gotta get going."

"Not so fast," Nevers said softly. "There's still no sense to it, Joe-Bob. You better tell me everything, the whole story. What the hell's going on? Why would Sully have it in for Brady?"

Joe-Bob hesitated.

"Come on, boy. You trust me or you don't. Time's wasting."

Joe-Bob's talk came halting and uncertainly now. Nevers's guess that Brady had sworn his weak-witted brother to silence was quickly confirmed as Joe-Bob unfolded the truth about how Cyrus had died. And about the recent cattle-stealing which Candler and Sully had broken up, followed by Sully's grim pledge to Brady. Nevers cut in frequently with questions, extracting the facts behind recent developments which had left him puzzled. So Brady had framed Bowie Candler for Cyrus's killing and then disposed of Candler — or thought he had.

It was easy to start drawing speculations as to why Brady, then Sully, had suddenly departed Chainlink this morning. Mere speculations. But meaty enough to make Nevers's deepening excitement balloon into a savage exulting. Jesus, yes. This could be exactly the situation he'd been waiting for.

"From what you say," he told Joe-Bob, "I'd hazard that breed means trouble for your brother. We best hustle and hope we're in time."

Joe-Bob blinked in surprise. "You coming?"

"For sure. Always told your pappy I'd watch

out for you boys. You, me, Trinidad, that's three guns, enough to handle anything needs doing."

They tramped back to the cutting site.

Nevers mounted his own horse and borrowed Barney's for Trinidad, merely telling the crew that something had come up and they'd be gone a while; Barney was left in charge of the detail. Afterward the three of them set a quick jogging pace toward the northeast. No point returning to headquarters, Nevers said; they'd shave off an hour by cutting Brady's trail where it entered the foothills.

Riding a tight anxiety, Joe-Bob pressed ahead of his companions. Nevers reined over close to Trinidad, saying quietly: "I figure there'll never be a better chance."

"*Bueno*. That is what I think. Now?"

"Not yet. I want 'em both. And it's got to look like someone else done it."

Trinidad raised his brows. "Ah. Sully?"

"Maybe. But I got a better notion." Nevers paused. "Mrs. Trapp told the kid it looked like Sully left with a sack of grub. What's that mean to you?"

"Maybe you better say it, Faye."

Nevers ticked off the points of what Joe-Bob had said: it added up, he thought, to possibilities that Bowie Candler was still alive, that Sofie Ekstrom might be with him, that Sully was fetching them food. Say Brady had figured out the same and had ridden up in the hills to confirm or refute the idea. Say Sully had figured out

251

what Brady was up to and had gone to get ahead of him and deadfall him. All this was guessing, but Nevers thought the pieces fitted together.

Even if his guesses weren't wholly right, this looked like a prime opportunity.

How many people knew that Brady had left Bowie Candler for dead the other night? Only the Trapp brothers and the two of them. Brady had told everybody that Candler had fled into the mountains after killing Cyrus. All right now. Suppose it could be made to appear that today Brady had gone up there looking for his father's killer. If everyone knew there'd been no love lost between Brady and Cyrus, they also knew there was bad blood between Brady and Candler: reason enough for Brady to go hunting Candler alone.

Only suppose when he found him and they traded shots, it was Brady who was killed. And suppose that moments later Joe-Bob and Nevers and Trinidad had come on the scene and shot it out with Candler — and both he and Joe-Bob were killed.

Trinidad pursed his lips, nodding. "We follow Brady's tracks, we find Brady. Then we fix both brothers dead, huh?"

"Simple as that. Simpler, if Sully's fixed Brady for us."

"But Candler, we don' know we'll find him. You just guessing he's alive."

"All right, say he ain't, say Brady did finish him two nights ago. But say he's alive, whether he drops out of sight or shows up later, it'll be the same. Our story's that Bowie Candler killed both the Trapp boys, maybe with his friend Sully's help. Be a hot day in January before anyone can prove different."

Trinidad began to show his teeth. Then the grin faded. "But the woman. Suppose Candler *is* alive and they're together?"

"Why," Nevers said gently, "in that case they'll be dead together. Maybe I had you wrong. Figured you'd do about anything to become foreman of Chainlink."

Trinidad showed all his teeth then. "You were not wrong, *amigo*. I am with you. Is just I want to get her all straight. And Sully, we run into him too, it's all the same, hah?"

"That's the picture. No witnesses."

No witnesses.

Part of Nevers's mind could coldly wonder at the insensate savagery of his own determination to carry the whole business exactly as far as need be. Yet he knew himself well enough to admit that if such an opportunity had been presented him any other time in his life, it would have been no different. Just a matter of recognizing the main chance and having the guts to seize it.

His moment had come when Adah had revealed the contents of Cyrus's will. And with it had come decision, cold and instant. Both Trapp sons must die. Their deaths might get the will thrown into probate, but the outcome seemed certain. Cyrus had no other close relatives. Adah would have Chainlink. And he would have Adah.

Getting Trinidad aside for a private discussion last evening, Nevers had put it to him just that way. Nevers had watched the man for years. He was as amoral as an alley cat; his friendship for the Trapp boys was only skin deep. With his reckless *pistolero* years behind him, Trinidad had an eye to the modest ambitions that a man of his race might realize in a gringo world; what better might he hope for than the foremanship of Chainlink? It was simple. All he had to do was help ensure that the next owner of Chainlink would be Cyrus Trapp's widow. Nevers couldn't say how or when; Trinidad would have to keep alert and be ready to follow any cue at a moment's notice.

Trinidad had done well so far.

Joe-Bob dropped back beside them, his face twitching nervously. "Snow's going fast, Faye — we gotta pick it up before them tracks is melted away."

"All right, kid. Let's pick it up."

They quickened pace. In a half-hour they angled across Sully's horse tracks and, a little farther east, onto Brady's. These they followed north into terrain that climbed steadily, and then the trail bent sharply west. Nevers was puzzled for some minutes till he realized that Brady had turned toward the old line camp. Which might have been a shrewd guess on Brady's part.

Suddenly Trinidad drew rein and pointed.

254

"Faye — look there!"

Nevers followed his pointing hand. On the slopes above them, the long trail up to the line camp wound in and out of sight among pine groves and across bare shale promontories. You could see parts of the trail from a long way off. And coming distantly into sight now was a party of three riders descending the trail, slowly and single file. Nevers dug his field glasses out of a saddlebag and trained them.

That was Brady in the lead. Were his hands tied in front of him? Bowie Candler rode close behind him, and then came Sofie Ekstrom. Nevers noted that Candler was riding Sully Calder's paint horse.

As he scanned, Nevers told his companions what he saw.

"Jeez," Joe-Bob said bewilderedly, "what's happened, anyways?"

Nevers shrugged. "Anyone's guess. Come on, let's get higher up. I know a good place to wait for 'em."

The place Nevers had in mind was a dense stand of pine at the base of a long snow-mantled slope where the trail snaked upward. Here he ordered a dismount, and the three of them concealed their horses back in the timber and took up a watch at its edge. Perhaps ten minutes later, Brady and Candler and Mrs. Ekstrom rode into view from the woods that crowned the rugged slant, picking their way slowly. Brady's head was sullenly lowered. Yes, his wrists were lashed together; he was a prisoner.

Suddenly Joe-Bob's horse released a loud blubbery snuffling.

The sound caused Candler to pull up sharply, peering at the trees below. They were still a hundred yards away, Nevers thought, but no help for it. Cupping his hands to his mouth now, he yelled: "All right, Candler, come on down here! We want to talk to you."

Brady lifted his head. If he didn't realize what was happening, he was quick to seize the opportunity it afforded. Giving a wild yell, he clapped his heels against his bay's flanks and lunged it downslope in a heedless run. Halfway to the bottom the animal's hooves skidded on melting snow; it pitched head foremost, flinging Brady ahead of him. The horse's cartwheeling fall narrowly missed Brady, who kept rolling head over heels, finally jarring to a stop. He lay where he was, stunned.

Candler was already hauling his horse around, yelling something at Mrs. Ekstrom. In a moment the two of them had vanished in the trees.

A faint smile hovered on Nevers's mouth as he tramped upslope to where Brady lay, Joe-Bob stumbling ahead of him. They pulled Brady to his feet, wet snow dripping from his clothes. Nevers took out a clasp knife and cut his bound wrists free. Brady's face had a pallid, shaken look; blood trickled from a gash on his forehead. Otherwise he wasn't hurt.

"Lemme be." He batted their hands away; his

256

gaze focused on Nevers. *"You?"*

"Uh-huh. Me. Joe-Bob told me the whole story. Everything. Thought you might need some help."

Brady swung his head, looking a raging question at his brother. Joe-Bob gave a small wretched nod.

"Don't be blaming him," Nevers said mildly. "I kind of wrassled it out of him. To repeat, we figured you might need help. Didn't you?"

Brady rasped a palm over his jaw, scowling. "Yeah — I sure as hell did. But Jesus. You?"

"Why not? My job's my life, Brady, you know that. It's pretty clear that if I want to keep it, I got to get on your right side. You're a Trapp, you'll try to hold Chainlink together. Am I right?"

"Yeah — sure."

"You got the feeling for it I got. Somebody else might split the outfit up and sell it off in chunks. I want to keep my place, I got to keep your ass out of prison. Does that make sense?"

Brady tugged his beard; his eyes narrowed. "Maybe. But just how far you willing to go?"

"Far as need be," Nevers said calmly. "We'll have to tend to Candler and the woman, you know."

"Yeah — track 'em down." Brady's gaze turned indrawn and vicious. "Candler for sure."

"Both of 'em. The Ekstrom lady can carry tales same as a man. You can trust Trinidad here. He's with us."

"I can see that," Brady snarled. His glance

swiveled upslope to where his bay stood, reins trailing, trembling but unhurt. "Let's quit jawing and get going. I get first shot at that pilgrim bastard — don't forget it."

CHAPTER EIGHTEEN

As he and Sofie rode back up the twisting rocky trail with reckless haste, Bowie was cursing in a quiet, monotonous, bitter tone. It was pure luck that a horse's snuffling had stopped them from riding into the jaws of a deadfall. But he had nobody but himself to blame for letting Brady break away. If he hadn't been startled totally off guard by Faye Nevers's shout, Brady wouldn't have made it. They could have used him as a hostage to get by Nevers and anyone with him.

Nevers might have come up here alone. Or he might have had others with him in the trees. Unable to tell which, Bowie hadn't hesitated to turn tail. And the only way to retreat was up the trail they'd just descended. Of course he couldn't be sure of Nevers's intent, but summing up what he knew of the man, it seemed logical to suspect the worst. Considerations of justice or loyalty wouldn't mean a damn to Nevers; whatever had brought him up here had to involve some private ax he was grinding.

So it made plain sense to get clear of the man. If he'd misjudged Nevers, he'd be made aware of it soon enough. For unquestionably Brady would want to hunt Bowie Candler down. What would Nevers want?

He halted; Sofie pulled up beside him.

"They'll want me if they want anyone," he

told her. "You stay here."

"I go with you, Bowie. Wherever you go. Don't you know this now?"

"They won't hurt a woman," he said harshly. "Not unless they catch up with me and you're along. Then they might not give a damn if you're in line. You understand?"

"I understand. But it doesn't matter. I go where you go."

To her it was that simple. Bowie gave a soft angry groan. He growled: "All right,, come on. We are going to make time, and if you can't hold up, I'll have to leave you."

"*Gud bevara* — how tough you talk." Her lips curved up at the corners. "I can hold up. But if I could not, you wouldn't leave me. Go on — go on now."

They moved at a brisk pace up the trail until the buildings of the line camp came into sight again. Here the trail ended, and Bowie had the bleak thought that if they went on, they'd be heading into terrain unknown to him, country where pursuers would have all the advantage. But did they have a choice?

Motioning Sofie to halt, he sat his saddle and pondered their situation. The afternoon was deepening, long sun rays gilding across the snow-sided peaks with a pale lemon glow. Striking across the unknown range to the north at this time of year would be foolhardy, he thought. Just the notion of getting caught by a blizzard on those rugged peaks made him

260

queasy. Over west a ways, they could have cut across through the passes he had followed from K-town, but from their present vantage they'd have to set out blindly. Best chance, it seemed, was to circle into the ridges and then down to the Oro River valley and on to Saltville. He didn't have Brady, but he did have the truth, and the sheriff would listen. No chance of reaching Saltville before tomorrow; that meant a night of camping out.

Dismounting, Bowie went into the cabin and stripped the bunks of blankets. He rolled them together and lashed them to the cantle of his saddle. A lot of the thin snow cover had melted off today, but what remained was enough to permit easy tracking. *Would there be a pursuit?* That was something he wanted to be sure of before he and Sofie went much farther. He led the way down an easy graded slope back of the line camp, and dipped into a long timbered vale.

Ten minutes later they emerged from the timber as the land climbed to another barren-looking ridge. At its summit Bowie halted and got out his old army binoculars, which had served him well in his horse-hunting days. He trained them on the line camp at the crown of the ridge they'd quitted.

Yeah — there they were. Four of them. He identified them easily. Brady, Joe-Bob, Nevers, Trinidad. That pretty well answered it, he thought. It didn't matter what their individual motives might be. No party made up of those four boded any good for him.

Already they were following the tracks into the timbered dip, and there was no time to lose. So far Sofie had followed Bowie's lead unquestioningly. Now, as they picked their way across the ridge to its other side, he told her how he had the situation sized up. Best hope was to keep ahead of the Chainlink men till nightfall. With any luck they could keep on going for a time after the failing light forced the pursuit to halt.

For the next few hours, Bowie continued a gradual swing toward the west, climbing steadily higher but not wanting to penetrate far into the mountain range. As it was, they were swinging around the northernmost foothills, brushing the base of a great top-squashed peak. Sunset was bleeding horizontally along the rim of earth, its pink rays flaming across the south slopes of the range. Dusk and darkness soon. And the last chance for escape. Bowie headed into a wedge-shaped cleft between shouldering ridges, pressing for speed in his worry that the men behind might be making better time.

Minutes later, he knew that he'd blundered Sofie and himself into a trap. The cleft angled out of sight ahead of them, but even before they'd made the turn and followed the passage to its end, Bowie had the sinking conviction that he'd boxed himself in. The premonition was right: the cleft ended in a blank granite cliff where the two ridges folded together. The sides were too steep and high to climb.

"Get out of here — fast!" he told Sofie.

Wheeling their animals around, they clattered back down the cul-de-sac. Even as they broke into the open once more, four men were riding out of a scattering of pines a few hundred yards distant. Coming on slowly and spreading apart as they came. Of course — they'd known. Had known of the false pass and that Bowie was bound to head into it once he was fixed in this direction.

Now he and Sofie were in a real bind. Boxed at their backs by a dead-end trail. At their right by tall bluff-faced ridges. Ahead, four men were advancing, rifles up. To his left lay the slow-rising base of the squashed peak. Bowie hesitated, and then one rider raised his rifle and sent off a shot. Powder snow geysered yards ahead of their mounts.

"Come on!" Bowie yelled. Clapped his heels against the paint's flanks and whirled the animal up the mountain slope.

As if on signal, the four riders broke into a concerted run. They were opening up with rifle fire, but Bowie knew that the chance of hitting anything at this range on running horses was practically nil. Up ahead of him mottes of young spruce made zigzags of dark green along the slope. At this height the day's sun had hardly affected the fresh snowfall; it spun in flaky swirls from under the horses' hooves as they lunged into the ascent of a steepening escarpment.

Then Bowie reached the first of the low, thick,

close-growing spruce; he reined the paint into them and piled off. Yanking Sully's .45-.70 Winchester from its scabbard, he dropped onto one knee, facing downslope. Sofie slipped to the ground and came running over to crouch down beside him.

"Down flat," Bowie snapped. "Can't fight off four men and worry about you too."

Obediently she stretched out on her stomach under the spruces. Bowie brought the Winchester to his shoulder and settled his sights on the first rider, Joe-Bob, as he poured recklessly up the slope. Then Bowie quickly lowered his aim and pulled trigger. He had nothing against Joe-Bob, but he might be as gun-handy as any other.

The horse shuddered and fell to its knees with a piercing whicker. Then crashed on its side, pinning Joe-Bob's right leg. He let out a chagrined wail of surprise and pain.

Brady, Nevers, and Trinidad scrambled off their animals and scattered for the shelter of granite thrusts which studded the slope. Bowie, firing as fast as he could lever the Winchester, sprayed up snow around Trinidad's legs as he ran for cover. Just as he reached a towering boulder, a bullet smacked into his leg. Trinidad went down into cover with a howling curse: *"Válange Dios!"*

Both Brady and Nevers had dropped down behind sizable outcrops, and Bowie held his fire now, waiting. On this open slope he could easily pick off either man if he showed himself. As they'd taken cover many yards apart, they would have to communicate by shouting; he'd be forewarned of any joint move against him. By now the whole mountainside was sheeted in a last fiery flush of sunset.

"Brady!" Nevers called.

"Yeah?"

"The light's going. Get dark enough he can't pick us out good, we can break cover and swing around to either side of him. Take him on two sides. What about it?"

Brady grated an assent that was almost unintelligible, as if grinding his teeth in a raging impatience.

They'd left Brady's Remington-Keene at the line cabin, but he seemed to have another rifle: Joe-Bob's, Bowie guessed. He and Sofie had one rifle. If Brady and Nevers reached the thin skirmish line of spruce, they could face him on equal terms.

Except there were two of them. Bowie felt Sofie's hand close tight on his arm, but she said nothing.

The minutes dragged by in aching silence, except for an occasional cursing groan from the Mexican. Even Joe-Bob, helplessly pinned by his dead horse, was quiet. The red light faded to dusky rose and then to beige-gray; dusk thickened.

Suddenly Brady's bear-thick form bounded out of cover and off to the right with surprising

265

speed. Running low and fast from rock to rock, hummock to hummock, so that Bowie had only fleeting glimpses of him in the blurry dusk. He tried to fix a bead; he shot twice and heard the bullets scream off rocks. In a moment Brady would be out of sight and circling up toward the spruces.

Bowie bore down on a tight bead as Brady flickered into sight again, this time leading Brady's faint shape with a careful precision. He fired. Brady staggered and went down on his hands and knees. Bowie held his fire now as Brady floundered to his feet, yelling "Faye!" with a note of pure panic.

Nevers hadn't even moved, Bowie realized. Just as the thought touched the edge of his mind, a rifle spewed orange flame in the gray seep of dusk. It was Nevers's. And he wasn't firing toward Bowie's position. Brady whirled as the slug caught him in the shoulder. Then Trinidad fired. Brady was catapulted backward by the slug's force as it caught him full in the chest. His body sprawled darkly against the pale slope.

"O God," Sofie whispered.

Joe-Bob found his voice. "Trin!" he screamed. "You, Faye, you killed Brady! My God, you killed him —"

"Candler!" Nevers's voice sawed coldly across the slope. "You hear me?"

Bowie was silent for a stunned moment, trying to digest this. Nevers and Trinidad together in a

266

play to get rid of Brady? "Yeah — yeah, I hear you."

"We don't want you. We want the kid. Joe-Bob. That's all. You and the woman can ride away from this. Get clear away. All right?"

"You sure you want a couple live witnesses walking around, Nevers?"

"You shoot too damn well," Nevers yelled back. "I might be next. I never counted on a stand-off like this. Let's both sides back off. You both get clear out of the country and keep your mouths shut about what happened here. I'll take your word."

Like hell you will, Bowie thought. For a moment he was puzzled by Nevers's willingness to let Sofie and him ride free. Abruptly the answer came to him. Nevers and Trinidad would give out a story that *he* had killed both the Trapps in this fight. Since Brady himself had already given out that he'd killed Cyrus, who wouldn't believe it?

"Sounds fine," Bowie called. "Only I got a better idea."

"Yeah? What's that?"

"Suppose you and Trinidad ride away from here instead. Leave the kid be. What about that?"

A long silence followed. Then Nevers gave a mirthless laugh. "Look, let's talk it over, all right?"

"You're talking."

"Well, it's damn hard talking this way. How

about coming down to meet me halfway?"

Bowie's throat felt cold and parched. "Sure. Step out and start walking."

"All right, sure, you do the same. Eh?"

"Just as soon as we even things out. You tell Trinidad to throw out his rifle. Handgun too."

Another humorless laugh. "All right. You hear that, Trin? Do it."

"Yeah, I hear." The voice was husky with suppressed pain; Bowie guessed his bullet had smashed a bone. Disarmed, Trinidad would be out of it. "You really want this, Faye?"

"Do it. Throw 'em out, both guns."

Trinidad's arm holding his rifle lifted above the boulder. "Way out!" Bowie called. The rifle spun away from the shelter and slapped into the snow. Trinidad's pistol followed.

"Start walking, Candler —"

Nevers's voice was like a steel rowel grating on flint. Slowly he rose to his feet. Bowie sized the bad light and the distance between them. Too far for a good shot. And Nevers would start firing the instant he was sure of the range. Well, it was an even chance.

"Bowie? No!"

Sofie clutched at his arm as he got up. He pulled her hand away and tramped out of the spruces and started downslope. The last daylight was gone, but Nevers's dark form stood out vaguely against the white slope as he slogged upward.

Stumbling and slipping on the rough snow-whipped slant, the two men closed the distance between them. Wind sliding off the peaks burned coldly on Bowie's sweating face. His rifle was clamped in his right hand; his whole arm ached with tension.

When he saw Nevers's arms start to lift, he didn't hesitate. Coming to a dead stop, he took quick aim. The two shots merged. Powder smoke bloomed and frayed away on the wind. Nevers's curse echoed thinly across the rock field as he fell to his knees. But he was barely hit, or had only slipped. Instantly he was up and plodding onward, levering his rifle and bringing it up to fire again. Bowie stayed where he was, waiting.

Yes, Nevers was hit. Staggering slightly as he came on now, firing as fast as he could jack fresh shells into the chamber.

Close enough, Bowie thought, and settled his eye along his sights, firing and working the lever and firing again, again, again, steadily and carefully. Shooting downhill in the near dark was a hard challenge, but he didn't surrender to the wild dogged fury that had seized Nevers as though more than his life were at stake.

A bullet drove Nevers off balance. He seemed to roll with its impact as a boxer would roll with a punch, somehow keeping his feet. But he was hard hit. He stood swaying, his rifle sliding downward. With a dragging effort he raised it again.

Bowie was already settling a bead. The

moment his sights hung steady, he shot.

Nevers was smashed off his feet, tumbling and rolling down the slope. Almost as soon as he stopped, he was floundering back to his feet. Bowie couldn't believe it. His sense of two serious hits on Nevers was positive. Yet he was rallying for another try.

Very carefully Bowie aimed and pulled trigger.

Nothing. The Winchester's chamber and magazine were empty. And Nevers was lurching on and upward while Trinidad was crawling away from his rock toward the guns he'd discarded.

Then Nevers's legs began to fold in midstride. He took a final straining step and pitched forward in the snow.

Trinidad stopped his laborious crawl. "Faye," he yelled. When no answer came, he resumed crawling.

"I can see you," Bowie shouted. "Stop there or I'll blow your head off."

He was pointing an empty rifle, but he didn't think Trinidad knew it. He was right. Trinidad let out one clear despairing curse. Then he came to a stop on his belly.

Bowie called up to Sofie, then trudged slowly down the long slope, a vast weariness dragging at his heels. He paused to collect Trinidad's guns and tramped on to where Joe-Bob lay pinned. Joe-Bob was weeping in broken husky sobs.

"Brady, oh Jeez, Brady —"

"He's dead," Bowie said harshly. "Like you

ought to be. Like you meant me to be."

Joe-Bob wagged his head back and forth, gulping miserably. "I didn't mean nothing. Brady worked it out and I done what he said. Trin and Faye, why they want us dead?"

Bowie glanced at Sofie as she moved up beside him, then looked back at Joe-Bob. "You can ask Trinidad. You'd be as dead as Brady if I hadn't been here. Be the easiest thing I know to just leave you like you are."

"Aw, Jeez, no —" Joe-Bob gave a hysterical whickering laugh. "You wouldn't do that."

"Depends on you. You can tell the sheriff just what Brady was up to. Or you can stay where you are."

"Jeez no, I'll tell him whatever you say, all right? All right?"

"The truth," Bowie said wearily. "Just tell him the truth."

He looked at Sofie beside him. Where she belonged, he thought, and wondered that he'd ever thought otherwise. Wind sliced at their faces. Icy wind and growing darkness and the side of a lonely mountain. He felt tired as hell and it seemed as though they were a long, long way from much of anywhere.

But it didn't really matter. It didn't matter at all.

The employees of G.K. Hall hope you have enjoyed this Large Print book. All our Large Print titles are designed for easy reading, and all our books are made to last. Other G.K. Hall books are available at your library, through selected bookstores, or directly from us.

For information about titles, please call:

(800) 223-1244
(800) 223-6121

To share your comments, please write:

Publisher
G.K. Hall & Co.
295 Kennedy Memorial Drive
Waterville, ME 04901